D1417608

j92
Gersh

Kresh. An American rhapsody.

DATE DUE

FEB 28 1990			

AN AMERICAN RHAPSODY

The Story of George Gershwin

JEWISH BIOGRAPHY SERIES

AN AMERICAN RHAPSODY
The Story of George Gershwin
PAUL KRESH

illustrated with photographs

LODESTAR BOOKS   E. P. DUTTON   NEW YORK

Permissions to reprint lyrics quoted in this book
appear opposite the Contents.

Copyright © 1988 by Paul Kresh
Library of Congress Cataloging-in-Publication Data
Kresh, Paul.
  An American rhapsody.
  (Jewish biography series)
  "Lodestar books."
  Bibliography: p.
  Includes index.
  Summary: A biography of the successful composer of
musical comedies, popular songs, symphonic works, and
the opera "Porgy and Bess."
  1. Gershwin, George, 1898–1937—Juvenile literature.
2. Composers—United States—Biography—Juvenile
literature. [1. Gershwin, George, 1898–1937.
2. Composers. 3. Jews—Biography] I. Title. II. Series.
ML3930.G29K7 1988 780'.92'4 [B] [92] 87-24469
ISBN 0-525-67233-8

Published in the United States by E. P. Dutton,
2 Park Avenue, New York, N.Y. 10016,
a division of NAL Penguin Inc.

Published simultaneously in Canada by
Fitzhenry & Whiteside Limited, Toronto

Editor: Virginia Buckley

Printed in the U.S.A.   W   First Edition
10 9 8 7 6 5 4 3 2 1

Frontispiece: George Gershwin, composer

for Penrod and Hugo

CONTENTS

CONTENTS

ACKNOWLEDGEMENTS

Every writer must stand on the shoulders of others, especially if he is writing about the life of a celebrated person. In preparing this book, not only am I indebted to those who have written about George Gershwin over the years, but I find myself more heavily in debt in this regard than usual. I do not think these pages would have had as much value or interest were it not for the help so freely and generously given to me by Gershwin expert and biographer Edward Jablonski. This generous man not only helped me to obtain material that is hard to come by, including his own out-of-print volume *George Gershwin*, but spent hours with me discussing this project. In addition, he placed at my disposal photographs from the Gershwin archives, of which he is caretaker. Mr. Jablonski has published several other books about Gershwin, including one he worked on with Lawrence D. Stewart called *The Gershwin Years*, and his later book, *Gershwin*, and these volumes teem with information on their subject.

Some of the best anecdotes in this book come from the writings of that poker-faced comedian and composer Oscar Levant, who both loved and admired Gershwin, saw him through humorous eyes, and was always ready to remind him of his faults. More serious accounts are to be found in *George Gershwin: Man and Legend*, the first biography of Gershwin, written by his friend and mentor Isaac Goldberg. Other books, articles, and archival sources were valuable as well; they are listed in the bibliography at the end of this book. But it was the time I spent with Frances Gershwin, to whom I was kindly introduced by her friend Manya Starr—the wife of my own friend and colleague Amram Nowak—that made me feel I was beginning to understand my subject. Kay Swift, to whom I was introduced by Edward Jablonski, was another wonderful source of information about George and of helpful insights into his character. And whenever I felt I was losing my way while working on this manuscript, I could find it again by turning to the best guidepost of all—the music itself.

These pages were written and revised during two separate stays through fellowships at the Virginia Center for the Creative Arts, where the staff provided an environment that made it possible for me to forget all other projects and responsibilities while I devoted myself to this one.

What none of the above supplied by way of wisdom and clear-eyed suggestions, Virginia Buckley, my editor, certainly did. My gratitude goes also to my good friend Jean Gould, who listened to every single chapter with infinite patience and supplied much wise advice; to my friend Penrod Scofield, who had to walk our wirehaired terrier, Hugo, on many a snowy morning while I fussed at the typewriter; and to my associate David Sanford, who was a constant source of help and sensible counsel throughout the stages of research and preparation.

AN AMERICAN RHAPSODY
The Story of George Gershwin

MY GRANDFATHER'S VICTROLA

When I was growing up during the years of the Great Depression in the hilly neighborhood of uptown Manhattan known as Washington Heights, my family decided to banish that magical machine, our windup Victrola, to my grandfather's room.

In its place of honor in the living room was installed a shiny, floor-length, walnut cabinet containing what was called a superheterodyne radio, which became the entertainment center (television was still a thing of the future). There was a conspiracy afoot to toss out the dear old Victrola altogether; only my tears and pleadings preserved the poor, battered object from getting thrown away with the empty cartons after my father died, and we all went to live in a rather cramped apartment. There I no longer had a room of my own, and I was assured there was no place for the phonograph except with Grandpa. The old man never wound it up or played a record on it in his entire life, but he used to let me occupy his quarters when he was out with his cronies, and it was there I began my pursuit of the endless adventure of discovering music, including the music of George Gershwin. I was about thirteen then, and busy discovering a lot of other things too, but it was in that musty, shadowy ground-floor back room that I used to play, over and over, the records stored on the shelves of the cabinet below the little doors that hid the horn of our old Victrola. It was a haphazard assortment of records—the "Italian Street Song" from *Naughty Marietta*, a lively number my mother used to like to hum along with as she cleaned house; gems from various Viennese operettas; Al Jolson singing a sentimental favorite of my father's when he had been alive, called "Sonny Boy"; and "The Merry Widow Waltz," which my father used to like to thump out on his sister's baby grand when we went to visit her by trolley car in the Bronx on Sundays. As for classical music, that was something my mother's sister used to listen to on the radio when The New York Philharmonic broadcast its Sunday afternoon concerts—which meant I wasn't allowed in the living room and had to walk around on tiptoe until the whole program was over.

Then one evening on "The Paul Whiteman Hour," I heard the orchestra accompanying a pianist who might have been George Gershwin himself playing his *Rhapsody in Blue*. I could hardly believe it! Here was music that spoke my language, composed in a style apparently invented just for me. It seemed to shift suddenly from joy to sorrow, from high spirits to self-pity and back again, just as my own moods did. I lived on chocolate milk for lunch in our school cafeteria for a week in order to save up the dollar needed to purchase a record of *Rhapsody in Blue* with the composer at the piano and Paul Whiteman conducting. I can still relive that afternoon when school was over, racing to the neighborhood music store, then trotting home; waiting what seemed forever for Grandpa to leave the apartment; rushing headlong into his room bearing my treasure; nearly dropping the highly breakable 78-revolutions-per-minute black-seal Victor disc in my haste and excitement; winding up the faithful old Victrola; changing the needle (it took changing, if I recall correctly, after practically every play); and putting on the *Rhapsody*. Yes, this was the real thing. And it was mine. I played the record over and over for days, until the rest of the family made me stop.

A few years later, I was among the many thousands of people who used to attend what came to be known as the Gershwin evenings at Lewisohn Stadium, a kind of Greek outdoor amphitheater high above the College of the City of New York, where I would someday be a student. There, seated on a stone step in the cheapest section miles above the stage I had the thrill of watching as well as hearing Mr. Gershwin himself at the piano, playing his *Rhapsody in Blue* and his *Concerto in F* accompanied by The New York Philharmonic. What a thrill! Those suave, silken melodies and nervous New York City rhythms seemed to float up to my perch from another world—a smooth-running world of evening clothes and sophisticated, elegant people. As I listened to the music, it seemed to offer the kind of life most people in Washington Heights saw only on the screen in a Hollywood musical on a Saturday afternoon at Loew's 175th Street— the whole American dream, complete with penthouse, convertible, and trips to far-off lands. At the same time, it sang of the city where I lived—the jangling traffic, the rattling overhead elevated train system (soon to be torn down), the teeming streets, the airless rooms in grimy tenements, and the raucous chatter of the Lower East Side at the turn of the century. What musical language was this? It seemed to sing away in accents as Yiddish as they were American, with a little soulful Russian sorrow thrown in. I longed to hear the *Concerto in F* again, but when I went to buy it at our neighborhood record store, the album turned out to be so far beyond my allowance that I had to acquire each record in the set of three, one by one, over a three-month period. In this way, I memorized the first movement before I came to own the second; and by the time I brought home the third and heard it a few times, I practically knew the whole piece by heart. At least I thought I did. It turned out, as with most Gershwin recordings in those days, that the music had been cut so it would fit onto the right number of record sides.

From the *Rhapsody*, the *Concerto*, and Gershwin's later works for piano and orchestra, along with the musical travelogues he wrote *(An American in Paris*, the *Cuban Overture)*, it was but a short step to his new full-length opera, *Porgy and Bess*. When it opened in New York in 1935 I was fifteen, and the aunt who listened to symphony concerts on Sunday promised to take me to see it if I would only finally pass algebra. At last I did, and my reward was a seat at the Alvin Theater for *Porgy*. Her verdict when the curtain came down was that it had been a pretty noisy evening. She called the music cacophonous (some of the critics said the same thing), but I was thrilled beyond words. Again I started saving up—this time out of street sales of a magazine called the *Saturday Evening Post*—until I could buy the record album, four whole 12-inchers made up of highlights from the opera sung by white opera singers instead of the black ones I had seen on stage.

Since those days of discovery, I have never tired of George Gershwin's music—the songs he wrote with words by his brilliant brother Ira and others, the tunes for the stage and the movies, the serious works he composed for the concert hall and the opera house. As I have continued to collect his music on recordings for nearly half a century, I have been especially pleased every time one of his works, shortened and tampered with by a lesser talent than his own, has been restored to the way he wanted it to sound in the American musical language he helped to invent. I never had the privilege of meeting him—I was seventeen when he died. But like so many others who grew up loving his music, I have always secretly felt that I knew him. When he died, I felt as if I'd lost one of my best friends. A few months later, there was a memorial concert broadcast coast-to-coast from the

Hollywood Bowl (such network broadcasts were a novelty back in 1937). Because of the time difference, the program wasn't heard in the East until quite late, and my teenage friends and I, who had stayed up to listen, found it was soon getting to be dawn. We decided to stay together and watch the sun come up. By the time I arrived home by subway, it was broad daylight. My aunt met me on the street. She refused to believe that I had stayed up all night just to listen to a Gershwin concert. "I can imagine where you've been," she said. "I understand these things. But your mother doesn't." When we reached the apartment, I found that my mother had locked herself into the bedroom. She refused to come out and speak to me. "You are making her old before her time," my aunt said. When my mother did emerge at last, she still would say nothing, but her red eyes told plainly enough how it felt to have an irresponsible, lying young man for a son. There was no allowance after that, and no money for Gershwin records or any other privileges, until I went out and got a part-time job after school to support the habit. At any rate, half a century later, I took it as a kind of personal triumph when in the winter of 1985 I was able to see his most important piece of work, his opera *Porgy and Bess*, at last take its rightful place on the stage of the Metropolitan Opera House in his home city and mine.

1

A Fifty-Year-Old Dream

It was a chilly Wednesday evening in the winter of 1985—the date was February 6. The crystal chandeliers floated up to the ceiling of the luxurious auditorium of the Metropolitan Opera House in New York City. The lights dimmed. Conductor James Levine signaled to the orchestra in the pit below the stage, the gold curtain rose, and the short, breathless overture that sounds like a racing train chugged the audience south to Catfish Row, Charleston, South Carolina, for the first Metropolitan Opera production of George Gershwin's opera, *Porgy and Bess*. For the composer's sister Frances—Frankie, as everybody calls her—and other members of the family, along with the friends, well-wishers, and lovers of George Gershwin's music who were there that evening, this was the fulfillment of a fifty-year-old dream. George had finally made it to the Met—the Mount Everest of opera for every aspiring composer. But the sad thing was that he hadn't lived long enough to take part.

To be sure, not only George but many who loved him

A dream comes true—*Porgy and Bess* at the Metropolitan Opera
House, February 1985   © 1985 **BETH BERGMAN**

could not be there. George's brilliant older brother, Ira, who had written the words for so much of his music—including a good many of the lyrics for this very opera—had died in Beverly Hills a year and a half earlier at the age of eighty-seven. Their mother and father were gone, too. And since November 1981, so was their kid brother, Arthur.

Yet as the author John O'Hara had once put it, "George Gershwin died on July 11, 1937, but I don't have to believe it if I don't want to." Millions of us all over the world who have loved George Gershwin's music, and who have never stopped wondering what exciting works he might have gone on to compose if he had lived, find it hard even now to believe. That music is so alive, it just doesn't seem possible that the man who created it isn't still alive too.

The dream of a performance of his only full-length opera at America's most important opera house had almost come true all the way back in the 1930s. Otto Kahn, a patron of the arts and one of the directors at the Met, had gone to the three great composers of popular music in this country—Jerome Kern, Irving Berlin, and Gershwin—inviting each of them to compose an opera for the Met. Only George had responded to the challenge. His plan was to compose a Jewish opera based on a famous Yiddish play by S. S. Ansky called *The Dybbuk*. In fact, he had done quite a bit of thinking about it, even setting down some sketches of the music, when he learned that an Italian composer had already obtained the legal rights to create an opera based on Ansky's play. The question of rights in adapting a book or a play for the stage or the movies is very important. Unless the work is so old that it has become a part of what is called the public domain, nobody can adapt it, publish it, or perform it professionally without the permission of the author or the author's estate.

George turned instead to another idea that had been in his mind for some years—to make an opera out of DuBose Heyward's novel about black life in Charleston, called *Porgy*.

Then in 1934 Otto Kahn died, and the other directors of the Met didn't think that a jazz opera, which is what they had been told it was, would be suitable for their immensely respectable opera house. Instead, *Porgy and Bess* first opened in 1935 in a theater on Broadway. It was presented as a cross between an opera and a musical comedy—a folk opera, George called it. Feeling that the public would get bored and restless if it went on too long, he cut quite a bit of the music, and all the dialogue that was originally supposed to be sung between numbers was spoken. Even so, the production was not exactly the hit of the season.

Now, fifty years later, with every note restored to the score, with a chorus of seventy voices, a cast of the country's finest black opera stars, and a running time of more than four hours—the kind of elaborate production most composers only get to dream about—*Porgy and Bess* still drew only mixed reviews. The *New York Times* music critic Donal Henehan reported that "the grand opera approach" sometimes "worked wonderfully . . . but at other times it exposed unnecessarily the opera's musical and dramatic weaknesses." Even so, the opera's severest critics, including those who had never thought highly of Gershwin's so-called serious music, had to admit that the man who had composed *Porgy and Bess* was one of the most remarkable men of music to be born in our time. He was a man who conquered the hearts not only of those who knew his songs from the musical theater, the movies, the radio, and the world of popular music in general, but from the concert hall and the opera house as well. The famed conductor Arturo Toscanini once summed it up in these words: "Gershwin is the only real American music."

Who was this boy from Brooklyn, this high-school dropout who finally made it to the Met? How did Jacob Gershovitz— the son of an immigrant Jew from Brooklyn, Morris Gershovitz, and his wife, the former Rose Bruskin—become the George Gershwin who broke the sound barrier that had long separated popular music from classical? Who wrote hundreds of tuneful songs and serious compositions that continue to delight music lovers everywhere? How did he come to write this music, which still sets pulses quickening and feet tapping whenever it is played? How did George and his brother Ira, who furnished the words for so many of his melodies, happen to go as far as they did? What kind of a journey was it to fame and fortune? What makes George Gershwin's music Jewish, what makes it American, and what makes it great?

It turns out to be quite a story.

2

From Gershovitz to Gershvin

On the day that George Gershwin was born—September 26, 1898—in the borough of Brooklyn, New York, telephones were still a novelty; phonographs were funny-looking contraptions with big horns that played wax-coated cylinders for a length of two minutes; radio and television did not exist. If you wanted to go to the movies, you went down to an arcade where you dropped a nickel into a machine, plugged a pair of earphones into your ears so that you could hear some tinny music, and turned a crank by hand. You saw jumpy pictures of trains, trucks, fire engines, cars racing each other down roads, a heroine being rescued by her boyfriend after the villain had tied her to the railroad tracks, and bathing beauties—pretty girls in very long bathing suits.

The music many people in America were starting to listen to on piano rolls and playing from sheet music was a syncopated kind called ragtime. Others, especially if they were older, tended to prefer the light operas of Victor Herbert, like *The Fortune Teller*, or minstrel shows, where white men in blackface sang comic songs about the topics of the day and danced jigs and cakewalks.

When Jacob Gershvin (the boy was named for his paternal grandfather, Yacov Gershovitz) arrived in this world, jazz was played mainly by black musicians, and you had to go down South to hear it. As for so-called serious music, that was for highbrows, people who spent their money on Caruso records—Enrico Caruso was the most popular operatic tenor of the day—or on opera and concert tickets. But what most Americans seemed to like best was sweet and sentimental.

Jacob was born in a stucco house on a street called Shedeicker Avenue, right across from the neighborhood synagogue. The family had only recently moved to Brooklyn from Manhattan. His father, who had not yet changed his name from Gershovitz to Gershvin, had come from St. Petersburg in Russia.

A story famous in the Gershwin family tells how Morris Gershovitz rushed forward to the rail of the ship that brought him to New York to get a good look at the Statue of Liberty and lost his hat, which flew overboard in a gust of wind. Inside the hat, it seems, was tucked the address of an uncle he was supposed to look up in Brooklyn.

As happened so often for all the Gershwins, a strong sense of humor kept Morris from becoming completely discouraged that day. Even though he couldn't speak a word of English, instead of feeling sorry for himself, he laughed off his bad luck and decided to hunt up the uncle, knowing only that he was a tailor somewhere in Brooklyn. First, though, the newcomer looked for a place to live. He rented a room on the Bowery, in Manhattan's Lower East Side. Then he went to a poolroom, where he won thirty cents in a game. Supplied now with plenty of carfare (in those days a subway ride cost a nickel), he started riding to Brooklyn and asking, in a combination of Yiddish and Russian, for Greenstein the tailor. There must have been hundreds of Greensteins in Brooklyn who were tailors, but somehow the search narrowed. Morris's quest by steam train across the Brooklyn Bridge led to a neighborhood known as Brownsville. By some miracle, he finally found his mother's brother there. Yet Morris kept his independence by going back to the Lower East Side that same night and staying on in his own room.

Now, Morris Gershovitz could have remained in St. Petersburg if he had wished. His grandfather had been a rabbi there. His father, a mechanic, was so good at his trade that he had been drafted to serve in the artillery under Czar Alexander II. This had given the family certain privileges, such as being able to travel freely throughout Russia, when the movements of most Russian Jews were restricted by law to an area known as the Pale of Settlement.

While in his teens, Morris had figured out that a way for him to earn a living was to become a manufacturer of tops for women's shoes. Still, as a young man, he had never been one for all work and no play. He spent much of his spare time at pool tables and card tables. Also—just as would turn out to be the case with his son George—he had an eye for attractive girls. When he met a young woman named Rose Bruskin, he knew that someday they would be husband and wife. Then the military draft threatened Morris, and rather than spend twenty-five years in the imperial army, he took off for the New World with his uncle's name and address inside the band of that ill-fated hat.

By another of those coincidences that seemed to favor him, Morris found out that Rose Bruskin, the very girl of his dreams, had also arrived in New York with her family. And as luck would have it, her father was the foreman of a factory that made women's shoes. Indeed, there just happened to be a job open in the factory in the very profession Morris had planned to enter in St. Petersburg. Having found a job in New York, Morris began taking Rose out on dates, and on July 21, 1895, they were married. It was a big, traditional Jewish wedding, attended by all their old friends from Russia. According to family folklore, among the wedding guests

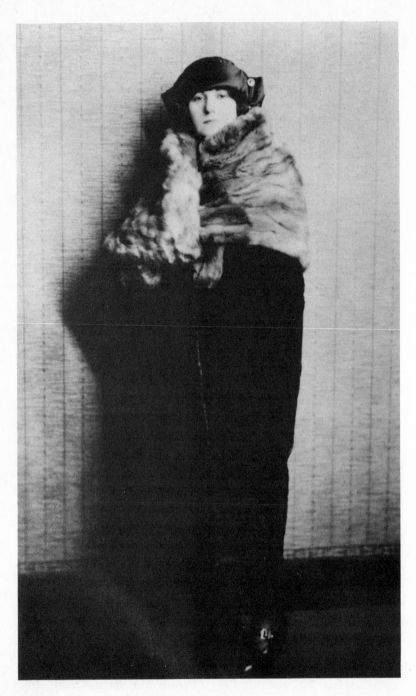

Rose Bruskin Gershwin

was the police commissioner of New York City, Theodore Roosevelt, who would later be president of the United States.

Morris didn't stay in the shoe factory long. He was determined to start a business of his own—and he went on starting new businesses for the rest of his life. At one time or another he tried running a restaurant, a Turkish bath, a bakery, a cigar store, a pool parlor, and a bookmaking establishment at a racetrack.

Morris and Rose also took up the business of raising a family. By then, they had changed their name to Gershvin. Their first son, Israel (later Ira) was born on December 6, 1896; in 1898, Jacob (later George); on March 14, 1900, Arthur; on December 6, 1906—exactly ten years to the day after Israel—the one girl, Frances (Frankie).

3

A Secondhand Piano

Morris liked to live near his place of business, so the family was always moving. In fewer than twenty years they lived in twenty-eight different places. After their marriage, Morris and Rose first settled in Brooklyn. George was two when the family moved from Brooklyn to the Lower East Side of Manhattan. In those days, just at the beginning of the twentieth century, this was very much a Jewish neighborhood.

According to Frankie, the members of her clan were a relaxed group, never too formal about anything, not even their names. George and Ira spelled their last name with a *v* for many years. When they decided to change it to a *w*, the whole family followed suit. Ira at thirteen had a fancy bar mitzvah, attended by two hundred people, in a kosher restaurant on Grand Street. Yet George, who always considered himself very much a Jew, if not a particularly religious one, never did have a bar mitzvah. In observing their religion, as in most things, the Gershwins were unusually permissive for the period.

The Gershwins never observed birthdays, either. It was only when as a grown man he applied for a passport to travel in Europe and had to obtain a copy of his birth certificate that Ira found out that his real name was Israel; since the family called him Izzy, he had always assumed his full name was Isidore.

The Gershwins were not rich, but they were never really poverty-stricken. Certainly they never went hungry. When things got tough, Ira would be sent out to pawn his mother's diamond ring. Frankie says she can never remember being without a maid. They were always on the brink of poverty, yet they never quite fell into it.

Rose, as Frankie remembers her, was a cool, far from overprotective mother, who let her children grow up pretty much each in his or her own way. Even as children they lived fairly separate lives. Rose was a shrewd woman, however, and kept a sharp eye on things. She enjoyed a busy social life and cared a lot about material things like clothes. As for Morris, he had a way of shrugging off troubles philosophically—making a joke rather than a tragedy out of whatever went wrong.

And so, in one New York neighborhood after another, going to one school after another, George grew up.

The city was a wonderland to him, a universe to be explored, an endless adventure. All his life he never stopped feeling that way about it. As a boy he roamed the teeming streets with their pushcarts and horse-drawn carriages, hearing the shouts of housewives on the Lower East Side bargaining for food and goods, the blare of Edison cylinders from music stores, the tinkle of pianolas from busy arcades, the roar of the elevated trains overhead, the squeals and curses of kids at play.

Yet when he was little, music didn't interest George at all.

An outing in the park: *left to right*, Arthur, maid, George, Rose, and Ira

"The only thing I ever played," he liked to say later, "was hooky." He also liked to steal a ride on a cart, to catch a hunk of dripping ice from an ice wagon, or to earn a cookie by watching a wagon for a driver.

Neighbors used to say things like, "You know, that woman has nice children, but that boy George—she's going to have a lot of trouble with him!" How would he ever make a living?

Frankie recalls that sometimes when George wanted to go to a movie, he would leave his shoes at home and pose as a penniless, barefoot orphan, begging one of the customers in line at a movie house to take him in. Sometimes he stole, too—fruit, fat pretzels, bagels. As for books, art, music— that was for "maggies"—sissies. Who could predict that someday this tough New York kid would write music that would thrill the world?

One day when he was six, while walking along 125th Street in Harlem, where the family happened to be living at the moment, George heard a sound coming from one of the penny arcades—a sound that brought him to a dead stop. He went inside and discovered a pianola mechanically thumping out a ragtime piece. Suddenly the music stopped. To hear more, he would have to drop another nickel in the slot.

George managed to come up with the right coin and put it into the machine. The pianola obliged him further by playing Rubinstein's "Melody in F" ("Welcome sweet springtime, we greet thee with joy. . . . ").

George stood there watching the perforated roll of paper glide over the tracks and the keys thump, and listened to the huffing and puffing of the mechanized instrument. He didn't know the name of the piece, but it certainly sounded beautiful.

The boy was transfixed. Then, as suddenly as it had started, the music stopped again. George continued on his way. But somewhere inside him the music went on playing. He could never get out of his head the fact that there was such a miraculous thing in the world as music.

Six years later, when George was twelve and had a reputation as one of the worst pupils at Public School 25 on the Lower East Side, he started to sneak out of the auditorium rather than subject himself to a recital by an eleven-year-old fellow student, a violinist named Maxie Rosenzweig. On the way out, though, he heard the sound of Maxie's violin. Just as had happened in the penny arcade, once again he stood stock-still in a kind of trance, as if a hypnotist had him under a spell. Maxie was playing Dvořák's "Humoresque," an extremely popular piece at the time. Again, George didn't know what piece it was or who had composed it, but he couldn't get over the beauty of it.

Years later, George remembered that moment in his life. "It was to me," he said, "a flashing revelation of beauty. I made up my mind to get acquainted with this fellow, and I waited outside from three to four thirty that afternoon in the hopes of greeting him. It was pouring cats and dogs, and I was soaked to the skin. No luck. I returned to the school building. Maxie had long since gone, he must have left by the teacher's entrance. I found out where he lived, and dripping wet as I was trekked to his house, unceremoniously presenting myself as an admirer. Maxie, by this time, had left. His family were so amused, however, that they arranged a meeting. From the first moment we became the closest of friends. We chummed about arm-in-arm; we lavished childish affection upon each other. We exchanged letters even when only a week and some hundred blocks lay between us."

They would wrestle and George would always win because Maxie was overweight and stocky, whereas George was lithe and lean and kept in shape playing stickball.

From Maxie, George learned a lot about music—about the great composers and what goes into making a musical composition. At Maxie's house on East 7th Street, George would try out tunes on the piano. George predicted to Maxie that they would grow up to be a great team: Maxie Rosenzweig on violin, George Gershwin at the piano. Maxie told George he didn't think George had it in him to be a musician. What did George know about music? All he ever heard at home were his father's Caruso records or his father playing tunes on a comb wrapped in tissue paper.

One day, while the Gershwins were living on Second Avenue over a music store, Rose Gershwin decided it was time for Ira to take piano lessons with his Aunt Kate. And so one morning a secondhand piano was hauled through a window of their apartment into the front parlor.

Ira dug in his heels and decided then and there that cranking the family Victrola was all the music making he was up to. Words, not music, were for him. He was fourteen at the time and more often than not holed up with a book.

All of a sudden, who should go darting over to the upright but the family delinquent, twelve-year-old George. He sat down and played through a whole song everybody happened to be humming at the moment, adding fancy embellishments of his own to the tune.

How could this be? Could a boy be born knowing how to play the piano without having had a single lesson? But George admitted that he had already been practicing on a pianola at a friend's house.

Ira was relieved of the burden of lessons from Aunt Kate. George was to take them instead. The family assumed that in a matter of weeks something else would capture George's fickle attention.

How wrong they were. That spring day in 1910 marked the start of one of the most remarkable musical careers in American history.

4

One Busy Young Man

As things worked out, it wasn't Aunt Kate who gave George his first music lesson, but a young woman from the neighborhood named Miss Green. Her lessons cost fifty cents each, but the family agreed that they were getting their money's worth. George took to the piano as though he had been born playing. For the first time he seemed to care about something. Before long, Miss Green felt she had no more to teach him. The same thing happened with two more teachers who followed.

Not that George had given up his other activities, which consisted largely of roller skating, taking part in street games and fights from which he often came home with a bloody nose, going to parties in whatever neighborhood the Gershwins were living, and exasperating his teachers in school. But music seemed to matter to him so much that it was agreed to let him go on with his studies under the supervision of a pianist he had met, a former bandleader and operetta conductor named Goldfarb. Goldfarb had a huge mustache and what George later described as a "barrel of gestures." George was so persuasive about the teaching abilities of Mr. Goldfarb that Pop Gershwin (the Gershwins and their friends always referred to their parents as Mom and Pop) agreed to put out the mighty sum, in those days, of $1.50 a week so that George could become his pupil.

"He started me out," George related years later, "on a book of excerpts from the grand operas. In six months I was advanced as far as *William Tell*." Nobody then ever dreamed that George, of all people, would someday go on to compose a famous opera of his own.

George loved watching his teacher's expansive gestures, but in the end he didn't learn too much from him. Meanwhile, in addition to all the other activities in his busy life, George also began to go to piano recitals. He even kept the programs and started putting together a musical scrapbook. He could also be found frequently at P.S. 63, attending, not classes, to be sure, but concerts by a group who called themselves the Beethoven Symphony Orchestra. Pretty soon, George, who always found it easy to make friends, had made still another, the pianist in the orchestra. He was a young man named Jack Miller, who thought the teacher he was studying under, Charles Hambitzer, might be the very one for George.

On a spring afternoon in 1912, Jack introduced George to Mr. Hambitzer. The new teacher invited his prospective student to play something for him. George, who all his life never had to be asked twice to play the piano, sat right down and launched into a fiery performance of the *William Tell* Overture. When he had finished, Mr. Hambitzer asked him where had he ever learned to play that way. Proudly George told him of his studies with the mustachioed bandleader. Hambitzer suggested that maybe they ought to see that fellow together and shoot him and "Not with an apple on his head, either," Mr. Hambitzer added, referring to the scene in the opera *William Tell*, where the hero is ordered to shoot an arrow at an apple that has been placed on the head of his own son.

Hambitzer, who had grown up in Milwaukee, where his father had run a music store, was an excellent musician. He knew how to play any number of instruments besides the piano, and set about trying to undo the harm that he felt earlier teachers had done to George's chances of becoming a good pianist. He taught George not only how to hear more in music, with his already well attuned ears, but the elements of music as well. For example, he placed George's fingers on the keyboard and showed his pupil that if he pressed certain keys down at the same time he would be creating a chord. He explained that a chord is one of the elements of harmony. Press certain keys, the result is a concord; press others, a discord.

As he continued to study with Hambitzer, George, by the time he was fifteen, had learned a lot about all the ingredients that go into the making of music: harmony, melody, theory, and much more. He discovered that it wasn't enough to toss his head back, look dreamy, and attack the keyboard with flamboyant gestures. He had to understand what was behind the notes he was playing.

George learned fast, and Charles Hambitzer was proud of his talented pupil. Hambitzer never took a penny for George's lessons. He wrote to his sister in Milwaukee, "I have a new pupil who will make his mark in music if anybody will. The boy is a genius without a doubt. . . ." He later told Frankie that George never watched the clock; on the contrary, he didn't seem to be able to wait until it was time for his next lesson. That certainly didn't sound like George. Maybe he wouldn't grow up to be a bum after all!

Instead, the young man was turning into a first-class student, at least so far as this one subject was concerned. George liked his teacher so much and thought so highly of him that he actually went out and rounded up ten more pupils for him. When Hambitzer died in 1918, just five years after George became his pupil, it was a terrible loss.

Meanwhile, George had already made an important discovery about himself: He would never be content if he confined himself to just one kind of music. He enjoyed the concerts he attended, and he was also crazy about ragtime, jazz, and the music of the theater. When he had an extra fifty cents he would spend it on a balcony ticket for a musical comedy. While still in his teens, he met a black composer and conductor named James Reese Europe, who had organized an operation called the Clef Club. Europe gathered black musicians from all over the world to form dance bands and orchestras. These groups went around playing jazz and other kinds of popular music in many parts of New York, especially in Harlem. Through Jim Europe, George became increasingly interested in the music of black America, in spirituals and in gospel music, and especially in jazz.

George also came to admire more and more the work of two popular American songwriters, Irving Berlin, whose "Alexander's Ragtime Band" was a big hit starting in 1913, and Jerome Kern. At a family wedding George had heard Kern's song "You're Here and I'm Here" and couldn't get over its lovely melody. On the one hand, then, there were the dreamy works of composers like Chopin and Debussy, and George couldn't get enough of them. On the other, there were the haunting tunes of Kern and Berlin, and jazz and ragtime, and he couldn't get enough of those either.

There was still another kind of music that, almost without his realizing it, stirred the soul of the young George Gershwin. This was the music of the Jewish people. George's family had never been devout, taking the same casual attitude toward religious observance as they did toward most other matters. Yet early on George had been exposed to the chants of the Jewish liturgy as well as to Yiddish intonations and expressions—the music of the Yiddish tongue that had been

Left to right: Ira, George, and Arthur, with a cousin

like mother's milk to Jewish immigrants who had grown up in Eastern Europe. As a boy he had seen his share of Yiddish musicals in the theaters along Second Avenue, heard folk songs and popular pieces that had grown out of the Hassidic chants of Poland and Russia, and whose melodies had traveled steerage class across the seas from lands as far off as Rumania. These tunes had already begun to echo in the popular music of America, and would find their way into his own as well. They were as much a part of him as the high-strung atmosphere, the intensity, the brash excitement, the longing for success that he absorbed as a boy growing up in New York.

All these elements would someday find their way into his own work.

Already, in addition to studying music, George in his teens was secretly trying his hand at writing some of his own. At fifteen he made up a song called "Since I Found You," with lyrics by a friend named Leonard Praskins. He also experimented to see what would happen if he applied ragtime rhythms to a classical piece. He put one together based on Schumann's familiar "Traumerei." He called it "Ragging the Traumerei."

In the years when George was studying under Hambitzer, his teacher had worried a little about his pupil's enthusiasm for jazz. He had wanted George to have a strong education first in the classics, to understand as much as he could about the technical side of music before experimenting with his own. One day in 1915 Hambitzer sent George to study musical theory with Edward Kilenyi, who had a fine reputation in the field, and who later became an important figure in the world of movie music (his son, Edward Kilenyi, Jr., went on to become a prominent pianist). Kilenyi, Sr., always spoke proudly of having been one of George's teachers, and of having predicted from the first a great career in music for him.

George studied under Kilenyi for five years and afterward often sought his advice on musical matters. For the first eight months he took two lessons a week with him. Kilenyi conscientiously taught him more fundamentals of music, taking up where Charles Hambitzer had left off. After several years, when he felt George was ready, he would invite performers from various orchestras to come and teach the basics about their instruments. The exercise books George kept in those days still exist. They show that he always wanted to be correct and neat. They also show that while he was willing to learn the rules, he was always trying to find new ways to express himself in music. Edward Kilenyi died in Florida in 1968. A few years before his death he appeared in a television documentary produced by the BBC, telling about his experiences as George's teacher.

As a teenager, George was one busy young man. Besides studying music, he often spent hours working in a restaurant Morris Gershwin owned at the time—one of a small chain of them Pop had somehow managed to acquire. George made $4 a week at the restaurant, but he hated the work, even when he graduated from the kitchen to the cash register.

George got himself a summer job as a pianist, playing popular songs at a mountain resort. Rose Gershwin wasn't pleased. She didn't like the idea that her son might become a musician. She thought he ought to be studying some practical trade like bookkeeping. What good would it be to eke out a living as a $25-a-week pianist? In truth, as Frankie recalls, all along Rose Gershwin, like many a mother ambitions for her children, had really wanted George to become a lawyer, Ira a doctor.

Somehow, George, in addition to all his other activities, was more or less attending the High School of Commerce. The only success he had there was when he played the piano for morning assembly. One day George came home and informed his mother that he was going to drop out of school altogether. He said he had met a man named Moses Gumble, who worked for a music publishing house, Jerome H. Remick & Company. George said Gumble thought he was a terrific piano player and was especially impressed by how well he could sight-read music. He had offered George a job at $15 a week at Remick's as a song plugger, one of the pianists who played new tunes in the hopes of selling the sheet music to people in show business.

Rose Gershwin said no and again no; Pop Gershwin found it the better part of wisdom to stay out of the argument altogether. George argued with his mother that $15 a week at Remick's was a lot more than $4 a week at his father's restaurant. If a life in music was good enough for the likes of Irving Berlin and Jerome Kern and Victor Herbert, why not for George Gershwin?

Confronted by such determination, Rose Gershwin finally gave in. On May 14, 1914, at the age of fifteen, George dropped out of the High School of Commerce to join what he regarded as the real world, in fact, the two worlds of music—classical and popular—and knew that somehow, someday, he would conquer.

5

Tin Pan Alley

If you walk down West 28th Street in Manhattan today, in the block stretching between Fifth Avenue and Broadway, you will see shops and drab-looking office buildings, a coffee shop, a photocopy service, an entrance to the BMT subway. No historic landmarks here. But in the early days of the twentieth century, this was a residential area filled with brownstone houses where people with moderate incomes made their homes. By 1914, on the May morning when George Gershwin set out to work on his new job, some of these houses had been broken up into little cubicles. In each cubicle stood a battered upright piano. When all the pianos were playing at once, you practically had to cover your ears to walk down the street without going deaf.

This block had come to be called Tin Pan Alley. Nobody knows for sure why, but one story goes that a journalist named Monroe Rosenfeld, passing the open windows on a summer day, heard all the pianos playing popular tunes at the same time and made the comment, "It sounds like some-

Tin Pan Alley and the Jerome H. Remick & Company music house where George plugged other people's songs

body pounding tin cans." Eventually, Tin Pan Alley became the nickname for the entire world of popular music, just as the words *Madison Avenue* came to stand, not just for a street where many advertising agencies had their offices, but for the entire world of advertising.

Tin Pan Alley was the world George was headed for as he hurried across 28th Street that morning. His job would be to

play tunes on a piano in one of the cubicles so that singers
and dancers and other show people in the market for new
songs, usually for vaudeville acts, could hear what they
sounded like. In those days people didn't go to their neighborhood theaters so much to see the movies, which were
short and silent with live musical accompaniments, as to
watch the vaudeville shows: the comedians, singers, dancers, and acrobats who made up the main part of the entertainment.

George's job was simply to put over a tune and convince
the performers that they wanted it for their acts.

So there, going on sixteen, sat George in his cubicle, plugging songs. He soon proved that he was especially good at
it—better, indeed, than anybody else. He could change a
song from one key to another or from high to low to make
it easier for the voice of a particular singer. He played with
such color, such energy, such enthusiasm that he made even
bad ballads sound better than they were.

Of course George's ambition in life was to be a lot more
than a song plugger. He dreamed of writing songs, songs
that would set the whole world humming and singing and
dancing, of writing the music for Broadway shows, even of
writing symphonies and operas. He could imagine opening
the day's newspaper and seeing his picture in it, next to
words of extravagant praise from a critic. He could imagine
himself living in luxury, too, maybe in a penthouse high
above the Hudson River on Riverside Drive, a dream he
shared with millions of other aspiring New Yorkers of the
day. Meanwhile, in shirtsleeves and suspenders, the young
man sat there thumping out tunes. (A cigar was not yet stuck
in his mouth, as in so many pictures and cartoons of him,
but that would come before long.)

Actually, a song plugger didn't spend all his time in the
little cubicle. He also got out to the theaters, hotels, and
restaurants where singers performed, even to the counter at
F. W. Woolworth where sheet music was sold. When George's

day at the keyboard was over, he and a colleague named Benny Bloom often hurried over to what was called a picture house, where, during intermission, they would show slides on the movie screen. The slides presented lyrics of brand-new Remick songs. As the words flashed on the screen, Benny would lead the audience in singing them while George thumped out the tune on the piano. The purpose of all this was to encourage people to buy the sheet music or piano rolls for songs they heard, songs like "Rebecca of Sunny-brook Farm." The popular music that people played then either came out of the horn of a scratchy windup Victrola, a mechanical music box, or was punched out by a paper roll winding through a mechanical piano. Or else they picked out a tune on their keyboard at home while the family stood around and sang the words.

Often on a Saturday afternoon George and Benny could be found at a department store called Siegel-Cooper, ten blocks down from Tin Pan Alley on 18th Street, distributing pieces of paper containing the words to Remick songs. Customers then gathered around George at the store piano and joined in the choruses. To make sure that they would be welcome at Siegel-Cooper, George and Benny took the trouble on these occasions to distribute little bottles of perfume to the salesgirls. Sometimes, on a good Saturday at the store, sales of Remick songs would top the thousand mark.

To make extra money, once in a while George would travel across the Hudson to East Orange, New Jersey, to make piano rolls. While the pianist played, a mechanism inside the piano would cut little perforations in a paper roll, which would later activate the right keys during playback. He was paid $25 for every six rolls he made. He did this for many years, sometimes under pseudonyms, inventing names for himself like Fred Murtha.

In the days when he was working at Remick's, George shared with several other talented teenagers his ambition to break into musical theater. One of them was a dancer who,

George during his piano-roll days

despite a thin and reedy voice, could put over a song in a way all his own. His name was Fred Astaire. Another was Fred's sister, Adele, a pretty girl with a mischievous sense of humor, who was also a terrific dancer; she was Fred's dancing partner. None of the three expected that one day George's half-joking prediction that he would write a musical comedy in which Fred and Adele starred would come true.

Fred and Adele Astaire, 1926

As the months went by, George was growing a little weary of plugging songs he considered second-rate. When George got bored enough with the tunes he had to plug at Remick's, the customers would be startled to hear suddenly pouring out of his cubicle a baroque melody by Johann Sebastian Bach. His partners would shake their heads in disbelief. Most of them played by ear and couldn't read music at all, let alone play the classics.

The young man who could play Bach on the piano at Remick's, who was still studying music, and who was so skillful at transposing music to fit the voices of his customers, soon began to attract the attention of people in the music industry and the entertainment world. The very men who wrote the songs often stopped by in person to hear George Gershwin play them.

Now George took the plunge in earnest from playing to composing. He started writing songs of his own. Often working until late at night, George began to jot down musical ideas in a notebook he called a tune book. Sometimes he would mark one of these "GT"—for good tune. More than a hundred of these tunes are now part of the Gershwin archives. One day he brought a couple of them to the head of the department that picked the songs to be published at Remick's. The executive listened carefully. Then he shook his head. No. His advice to George was to stick to piano pounding. Remick's had enough composers on its list already.

George, even then not one to sit patiently by waiting for life to offer him a break, decided it was time to do something about improving his prospects for success. Even though his job now included trips out of town to plug songs in places he had never before visited, George felt that he could no longer be satisfied selling the wares of others.

Another two years and the situation changed. George, now eighteen, and one of his friends, a young man named Murray Roth, had worked together on a song they called, "When You Want 'Em, You Can't Get 'Em; When You've Got 'Em, You Don't Want 'Em." George was sure this new song would break down resistance at Remick's, but it didn't. No other publishers seemed to be interested either. Then Sophie Tucker, one of the most popular vaudeville stars of the day, with a voice like gravel rattling in a pot, heard the song and thought it was just great. Her recommendation alone was enough for the Harry von Tilzer Music Publishing Company to agree to bring it out.

A few months after publication, George and Murray went around to see Mr. von Tilzer to ask after their royalties. He yawned, reached into his wallet, and handed over a five-dollar bill.

6

Family Portraits

When the Gershwins weren't moving so that Pop Gershwin could be near his place of business (one of George's biographers describes Morris Gershwin as having "the soul of the wandering Jew"), life for much of the family went its own way. Ira, who was often George's guide on bus and subway trips all over the big city, was working days in his father's latest business venture, a Turkish bath. But at night, when he wasn't attending evening classes at City College, where the tuition was free, he and George would go to see musicals, like *Century Girl*, or have dinner out, perhaps at a Jewish restaurant on the Lower East Side.

As a boy, Ira had loved to read paperback novels that cost a nickel—books like *Adventures of Young Wild West* and *Fred Fearnot*, which he had to hide because his parents disapproved of them. Later, when he discovered the public library, he became an inveterate reader. Books never meant that much to George.

In later years, Ira recalled his boyhood as a time of learning

Ira Gershwin, 1904

to swim in the Harlem River, of memorizing Italian phrases so that when he was ganged up on by Italian kids on Mulberry Street he could say the right password and avoid a sock in the jaw, which he sometimes got anyhow.

In his early teens, Ira went to high school at Townsend Harris Hall, a place known to accept only boys who were serious about their studies. There he began to show talent as a writer. He wrote a column called "Much Ado" for the school paper, and when he went on to be a student at City College he edited a column there too for the weekly newspaper the *Campus*. He was an admirer of a clever columnist of the day who signed himself with his initials, F.P.A. (they stood for Franklin P. Adams), and whose column in the *Evening Mail*, "The Conning Tower," was extremely popular. Before he was twenty, Ira had succeeded in getting one of his own contributions published in F.P.A.'s column. Then he made a whole dollar when he sold a story to the sophisticated magazine the *Smart Set* and began to believe he was really going to be a writer. He had to take a job as a shipping clerk in B. Altman's, a department store, however, to make a living. Then he worked as assistant to an uncle who was a photographer on Brighton Beach. Later he wrote theater reviews, three of them, for a small New York paper called the *Clipper*. When no more assignments came his way, he joined a traveling carnival as treasurer. At home again after many months, Ira had no clear idea what he would do next, but felt he ought to try writing lyrics for songs. He didn't know it yet, but he was on the verge of a career that would result before long in his becoming Mr. Words to his brother George's Mr. Music.

All their lives, George and Ira were as different as two brothers could be. George was outgoing, full of high spirits, ready for adventure, always with an eye for a pretty girl. He loved to be in the limelight and on the go. Ira hated to rise from a chair, liked peace and quiet, moved slowly when he moved at all. He was as shy as George was outgoing. George's clothes were dapper—in fashion; Ira was a conservative dresser. George was trim, tall, athletic, restless, always ready for attention. Ira was stocky. He hated to expend energy unless it was absolutely necessary, and if he could wriggle out of attending any social occasion, he preferred to stay home and read. Yet before long these two opposites would prove to be the perfect partners.

The first Gershwin to taste the life of the stage was their kid sister. Frankie says she grew up almost as an only child. For one thing, she was so much younger than Ira and George. As for Arthur, he went his own way. When George and Ira were older and worked as collaborators, they became closer, leaving Frankie pretty much out of their world. Frankie was a shy girl, but she had learned to dance and sing while she was still young. In 1917, Frankie appeared in a school recital and so impressed the family, as well as the audience at the Terrace Gardens on West 58th Street in Manhattan, that Rose Gershwin thought maybe the girl should go into show business.

When Frankie was ten, one of her mother's friends told Mrs. Gershwin about a producer in Philadelphia who was preparing a children's show to be called *Storyland*. Why not take her daughter down to audition for it? Off to Philadelphia they went. Frankie's act went over, and the producer of *Storyland* hired her. "The only reason my mother accepted this," Frankie says, "was because she came from Russia and wanted to see something of this country. When she heard we were going to Philadelphia, Boston, Pittsburgh, and Cleveland, she said, 'All right, we'll go.'" In *Storyland*, Frankie played a Russian dancer, coming on stage in a rose-colored velvet costume and dancing the steps traditionally reserved for men. "I was a big hit," she remembers. Soon Frankie and stage-mother Gershwin were traveling from town to town. Frankie was making a salary of $40 a week, more than any of her brothers. The fact that later Frankie failed to pursue a stage career as a singer and dancer was really the fault of her brothers—especially George. But more of that later.

The third of the Gershwin boys, Arthur, two years younger

than George, also showed musical talent. He started taking violin lessons, but after hearing George at the piano decided to give up. Like George and Ira, Arthur had a fine sense of humor. He complained, jokingly, that George could sit down while he took his piano lessons, but to take violin lessons Arthur had to stand. He didn't think it was fair. Arthur did play the piano by ear, but this wasn't really his strong point.

Frankie found Arthur the most amusing of her three brothers. "He would just look across the room with a certain expression," Frankie remembers, "and I would start to laugh."

Arthur, too, wrote songs: "Invitation to the Blues," "Slowly but Surely," "After All Those Years," "Blue Underneath the Yellow Moon," "No Love Blues," "You're More Than a Name and Address." He even wrote the score for a musical, *A Lady Says Yes*. But it was a flop, and so, unfortunately, were his songs. His tunes were never destined to be hummed throughout the years as were George's. He tried to make money as a stockbroker; but even as a broker he was broke more often than he was in the money, and he was always borrowing from his friends and his brothers. He and his wife, Vicki, did provide Mom and Pop Gershwin, however, with one thing they never got from George or Ira: a grandson, Marc, who grew up to follow in his father's footsteps by taking up a business career on Wall Street.

Another member of the Gershwin family who became a close friend of George and Ira was their cousin Harry Botkin, a young painter who lived with his family in Boston but often came to New York to visit. He, too, became involved with the music business when, in 1917, he sold the artwork to a cover for the sheet music of a song called "When Kelly Sang Killarney."

Indeed, an interest in the visual arts and a proven talent with paint and brush were not confined to Cousin Harry. Ira showed skill with pen and ink and did clever caricatures. George too was so good at painting that in the last years of his life there were several exhibitions of his works that were taken quite seriously in the art world. Frankie also took up painting and has achieved more than a little recognition for her work. And Pop Gershwin never stopped buzzing out tunes on his tissue-paper–covered comb. There was talent to spare in the Gershwin family! But as the great French artist Henri Matisse once said, "There are plenty of men with talent—only how many work at it?" George Gershwin worked at it. Ira did too, but George always had to keep after him.

7

Mr. Words
and Mr. Music

While he was still pounding the piano at Remick's, George was also storing up a number of tunes of his own. One was called, "You're the Witch Who Is Bewitching Me." The same tune with different lyrics later became the haunting song "Drifting Along with the Tide." With the lyricist Irving Caesar, George wrote a song that looked forward to the end of World War I. It was called "When the Armies Disband." And although Remick's didn't publish any of George's music while he worked there, after he left, in 1917, they did bring out a rag called "Rialto Ripples," on which George collaborated with another composer, Will Donaldson.

Even these early melodies bear George Gershwin's signature: Although the rhythms come from the ragtime music that was still popular and echo the sentimental love songs of the day, these songs already show signs of the originality, the sophistication, the natural feel for music that keeps so much of what George composed still alive while so many other popular tunes of the same period have been forgotten.

It was George's special hope that one of his songs would someday be sung on the stage. He didn't have to wait long for that to happen. It was a lively little melody that he contributed to a revue called *The Passing Show of 1916*. The fact that his very own tune was used for a production number in the show made George particularly happy.

Yet he was far from happy with his job at Remick's. He was getting tired of playing other people's songs. "Perhaps," he said later, "my ears were becoming attuned to better harmonies." And so, after four years at the place, one morning he marched into the office of his boss, Moses Gumble, and announced that he was quitting.

Mr. Gumble didn't seem terribly surprised by the news. He was sure George was destined to do better things at a piano keyboard than put over tunes by other composers.

Even so, after he left Remick's, George felt empty and lost. He had no idea what he was going to do next. Although he was never a man to look back and wring his hands over a decision, the future looked bleak.

After several weeks of being idle, George heard there was an opening for a pianist at a theater on 14th Street. He was hired to tinkle away at the keyboard while the other musicians went off to supper.

George was getting along fine at this new job until one night he was asked to supply the accompaniment for a new act that involved two lead singers, a comic, and six chorus girls. It was up to George to keep track of the music for all of them and to come in exactly at a number of complicated cues. That night occurred one of the most embarrassing moments in his professional life: He missed a cue! George could feel his cheeks turning red. He wondered if there was anybody out there he knew.

Missing a cue was bad enough, but there was worse to come. Suddenly George heard the comedian in the act shouting across the footlights, "Who told you you were a piano player?"

George couldn't wait for the curtain to come down so he could slink out into the night. He never even stopped to collect his pay.

What to do next? He tried to make some money playing the banjo at parties. He worked with a band in a nightclub. Nothing seemed to be leading anywhere. For George Gershwin, this was even worse than it might have been for most young men his age. Nineteen and still not famous! He couldn't forgive himself. But another job came along, a job with a real Broadway show this time, called *Miss 1917*. What made the whole thing exciting was that the music for *Miss 1917* was by Victor Herbert and by the composer of the day whom George most admired, Jerome Kern. Here would be a chance to find out how a show was made ready for Broadway—to be a part of it—and to play songs by the very songwriter whose work he loved best, and even to meet him in person.

Meet him George did. And there was another pleasant experience in store. At the same theater where *Miss 1917* was playing, the Century, Sunday night concerts were also held. At one of these the star of *Miss 1917*, Vivienne Segal, who was destined to become one of the brightest stars of the American musical theater, actually introduced two of George's own songs. One was "Yoo-oo Just You"; the other had the even sillier title, "There's More to the Kiss than the X-X-X," complete with kissing sounds. Remick's published the song, which gave George additional satisfaction.

Even with all this newfound success, there was no spare money jingling in George's pocket. Luckily he still lived at his parents' home; he couldn't have gone far on the royalties he was getting from his music. What extra money he made he earned at the piano, playing for rehearsals, playing for a while in a show orchestra, playing for singers in vaudeville troupes.

All this George regarded as small time, and small time was always too small for George. He craved to be involved in something really big. He didn't have to wait long.

Two great talents—George Gershwin and Jerome Kern

One of the most popular singers during the period was Louise Dresser. She had heard of George's talent from show business colleagues and sent for him to offer him a job as her accompanist on a vaudeville tour that would take them to Boston, Baltimore, and Washington, D.C., after the New York opening. George leaped at the chance. One night during the tour, just before America entered World War I, President Woodrow Wilson turned up in the audience at the Washington, D.C., theater where the show was playing. George and Louise returned the compliment by marching together in that week's preparedness parade.

In the daytime, George practiced the piano a lot, but he also found time to go on writing songs. He was more impatient than ever for success. He had only published four songs, which didn't seem to him to add up to much. His next songs had words by three men who became famous for their lyrics but who were not yet really regarded as professionals. They were Irving Caesar, Lou Paley, and George's own brother Ira. Caesar was still making a living by working in an automobile factory, Paley was a teacher, and Ira was at the time working in his father's Turkish bath. But Ira was getting tired of turning his hand to so many jobs that led nowhere. Maybe the future was not out there in the world of carnivals and his father's shaky business enterprises but right at home with his own brother George.

Ira was having trouble in school, too, being defeated by the math and chemistry courses at City College. As calculus loomed in the immediate future, he decided it was his turn to drop out of school.

The family was bitterly disappointed. His mother had simply assumed that with George lost to music, Ira at least would grow up to be a doctor. For a while Ira just drifted along, escaping at the movies and reading "without plan or purpose." Then all at once he began scribbling down words for a song George might set to music. "I started on the chorus. I wrote one. Discarded it. Wrote another. Started a third.

Wastebasketed all. . . ." But Ira did not give up until he had put down on paper a set of lyrics he felt were good enough.

Then George tried to put Ira's words to music. At first the lyrics and the tune would not work well together. But the two Gershwins, as they would for years to come, sat—George at the piano, Ira at a table in the family apartment—sweating over the words and the music until they knew they had actually written a song. They called it "The Real American Folk Song."

Ira signed the lyrics "Arthur Francis," using the first names of his sister and youngest brother. This was to be the signature he put on his lyrics for some time to come. He used the made-up name to avoid being accused of trading on his brother's, which was already beginning to be well known. For a number of years, whenever anybody wanted to meet Arthur Francis, George would say, "Mr. Francis is too busy to be disturbed."

"The real American folk song," the chorus went, "is a rag,/ A mental jag,/A rhythmic tonic for the chronic blues. . . ." This was just the sort of lively line George liked best to set to music, and the words and music are as snug together as a hand in a well-fitting glove.

Now, it so happened that at the time—the year was 1918— one of the most popular women of the vaudeville stage, a star named Nora Bayes, had chosen George's song "Some Wonderful Sort of Someone" for her latest show, *Ladies First*. George, who was never shy, asked her if she wouldn't like to have "The Real American Folk Song" in the show too. Miss Bayes ended up taking not only both songs but also George along with them as her accompanist.

To hear his lyrics during the tryout of *Ladies First* meant that Ira would have to travel all the way to Trenton, New Jersey. For a man of Ira's temperament, such a journey could be regarded only as a nuisance. Even so, he took the afternoon off from the Turkish bath where he was still working, got all dressed up in a green suit, purple shirt, and blue tie, reached the train somehow, and arrived in New Jersey. However, he managed to get off at the wrong railroad station and had to take a trolley car to Trenton. Ira did appear at the theater in time to hear Nora Bayes sing his lyrics that day. But when the show finally reached New York, "The Real American Folk Song" had been cut out of it.

During the six-week tryout of Ladies First, George and Nora didn't get on too well. She blamed him whenever anything went wrong. She found his fancy playing too complicated and said it threw off her singing. For his part, George was stubborn and would never change a single note he had written.

At one performance of Ladies First was a twelve-year-old boy who had come to see his uncle, Oscar Radin, conduct the orchestra. He sat in the gallery and was especially fascinated by George's work at the piano. The boy was Oscar Levant, destined in later years to become a familiar figure in George's life.

Ready for Adventure

One day George simply left the show and went back to New York. Actually, he had an ace up his sleeve. Before he had signed up for the tour with Nora Bayes, he had also put his signature on another piece of paper, a contract with the music publisher T. B. Harms.

A company executive named Max Dreyfus had heard George's songs. He didn't offer to publish any of them, but he did agree to hire George, not as a song plugger but as a composer! Harms would pay George $35 a week, a pretty substantial salary in 1918, and all George had to do was come in now and then and bring a new song with him.

It sounded like a fine arrangement, but six months passed before Harms actually published a song Gershwin wrote. That song was "Some Wonderful Sort of Someone," which had led to the meeting with Nora Bayes and the tour George had just abandoned.

When George went back to see Max Dreyfus, he was not in a good mood. All he could think of was that he had now reached the age of twenty, and he had published "only" five songs.

"George," said Max Dreyfus to the glum young man that autumn day in 1918, "how would you like to write songs for a musical comedy?" The show Dreyfus needed the new songs for was a musical revue to be called *Half Past Eight* (the time when the curtain used to go up in New York theaters.) George was a little disappointed because it wasn't a "book" musical, a show with a story rather than a collection of skits and songs. It was a pretty big affair though, as musical revues went in those days, with scenery, and even a couple of songs imported from Paris. George, who roused Ira long enough to help out with the lyrics for one of the songs, worked fast, secretly impelled by the dream of his name in lights on the marquee of a Broadway theater, on posters, in newspaper advertisements: "Music by George Gershwin."

Unhappily, even though *Half Past Eight* starred the big-name comedian Joe Cook, it was not exactly a winner. The show couldn't even live up to its name. On opening night in Syracuse, New York, the curtain didn't go up until a quarter to nine. The Broadway chorus that was supposed to sing in the show turned out to be nonexistent; all in all, the audience didn't feel they were getting their money's worth.

It was George's idea to send out Joe Cook and the other comedians in the cast carrying Chinese umbrellas to serve as the "chorus" and liven things up in the second act. The umbrellas, however, were cheap paper affairs and three of them just wouldn't open. The audience booed and hissed.

During the first matinee that week, some of the actors refused to go on at all unless they were paid. George was told to perform instead and play a few of his hits. As he liked to point out when he recounted the story in later years, "I didn't have any hits." Needing a shave and wearing a rumpled blue suit, he went out to the piano and played a few of his tunes. The audience sat on their hands. Stony silence.

Half Past Eight was a gigantic flop. It got terrible reviews except for the songs by George Gershwin. The critics found those delightful. Eventually George managed somehow to worm enough money out of the management for the fare home. "It was a good experience for me," he used to say. "I got a thrill on seeing on the billboards 'Music by George Gershwin'."

Only a year later, at the age of twenty-one, George was again to have the thrill of seeing his name on a billboard. This time the show was *La La Lucille*, a real musical with a story, not a revue. This time not just a half dozen songs, but all of them, were by George Gershwin.

The producer was a man named Alexander Aarons. He had heard one of George's songs, "I Was So Young (You Were So Beautiful)," which had found its way into a musical called *Good Morning, Judge*. He was the manager of a clothing store, but his father was a producer and Alex hoped to follow in his father's footsteps and make good in show business. He decided to give up the store, produce a musical himself, and ask young Gershwin, whose song he had liked so much, to write the music for it. Alex's father thought he was out of his mind. Why ask an unknown composer, when he could get Victor Herbert or Jerome Kern? But Alex chose George.

Although George had not come to him for help, Jerome Kern's influence on some of the songs in *La La Lucille* is clear if you know the music of both men. Songs like "From Now On" certainly show that influence, though other songs in the show, like "Nobody But You," which George had written while he was working at Remick's, are unmistakably his own. *La La Lucille*, in fact, was in every sense a success. It ran for 104 performances at the Henry Miller Theater on Broadway.

Another development in George's life occurred when Irving Berlin came to Harms's one day, where George was still working, with the thought of leaving his old music publisher and having Harms publish his songs instead. Berlin had brought along a new number called "The Revolutionary Rag," his response in song to the recent Russian Revolution. Max

Dreyfus asked George to run through it. "He sent this kid in," is the way Berlin later told the story. "I couldn't hear my own tune—but it was brilliant." The reason Berlin hadn't been able to hear the tune was that George was up to his old song-plugging tricks, adding all sorts of harmonic decorations in order to put the tune over. Before Berlin left, he invited George to sit down again and play some of his songs. He didn't have to ask twice! Berlin was so impressed by what he heard that he invited George to come to work for him as a kind of musical secretary. The truth is, Berlin could not write music too well and even had a piano especially adjusted for him so that everything would come out in the same key, while George was already rapidly becoming a sophisticated master of the keyboard and of musical composition. Berlin certainly could have used a young man of George's skills. But George said no.

In the map of every life, there are certain crossroads, and the road one chooses can be terribly important in determining where that life will lead. Even though they followed separate paths, the two men pursued a warm friendship that lasted for the rest of George's life.

In his twenties, George was always ready for adventure. He never tired of going to parties, had many girlfriends, and loved to travel.

Once he accompanied Al Jolson, the Broadway star who would later become world famous for singing "Mammy" in the first all-talking picture, *The Jazz Singer*, on a vacation trip to New Hampshire. It was a journey of a day and a half by train. The idea was to get some rest from the pressures of big-city life and take walks in the woods. But George, ever the nervous, energetic city boy, couldn't stand the peace and quiet of the country and decided to head for home. Only the long train trip back seemed like a big ordeal. On a dare from Jolson, he agreed to fly, at a time when airplanes were far from being a common form of public transportation. George was always a little ahead of his time.

After *La La Lucille*, George wrote several songs for use here and there in other shows, but he hadn't yet written the kind of big hit that makes a composer famous. Then the lyricist Irving Caesar came to him with an idea for a song. A dance known as the one-step was sweeping the country. The latest one-step song to go over with the public was called "Hindustan" and had an Oriental flavor. How about writing a one-step with a genuine American flavor? George and Irving talked about it over dinner at a popular show-business restaurant named Dinty Moore's. Afterward they took a bus up to the apartment on Riverside Drive in Washington Heights where the Gershwins were living at the time. When they got there, they found a poker game going on.

George and Irving went into an alcove beyond a beaded curtain and settled down at the piano to work on the song, about a river in the South named the Swanee. This river never existed but is better known than some that do.

"Boys, finish it some other time," the losers in the game kept saying. But the collaborators, encouraged by the winners, went right on until the song was finished. Then Pop Gershwin appeared on the scene to accompany George on his comb, covered with fresh tissue paper, while George sang the words: "Swanee How I love you, How I love you/My dear old Swanee. . . ."

Nobody paid much attention to "Swanee" when it was sung as part of the stage show at a new movie palace in Manhattan called the Capitol Theater. But when Al Jolson sang it in blackface in the Broadway revue *Sinbad*, "Swanee" became a hit. Jolson's record of it sold a million copies. The sheet music sales were staggering. Nothing else George ever wrote would be such a huge commercial success.

And so the dream of conquering at least one musical world, the world of popular music, was already coming true for George. Meanwhile he continued jotting down musical ideas in his little notebook. From these notebooks would come some of the most haunting melodies and appealing musical works of the twentieth century. In one book he put down more than sixty ideas in the space of forty pages.

9

The Jazz Age

The year 1920 saw the beginning of the period in American life that has come to be known as the Jazz Age. It was a time of prosperity, a time when liquor was banned by law—the Prohibition—and people drank in secret and in private bars called speakeasies. It was a time of fast automobiles and short skirts, when women painted their nails dark red and smoked cigarettes in long holders, bobbed their hair, and wore heavy makeup. It was a time following World War I, when many people rebelled against the old conventions and devoted much of their lives to pleasure.

The music of the age was jazz, which had been developed by black people in the South but gradually spread over the entire nation and eventually throughout England and Europe. Jazz gradually replaced the ragtime George had heard in his boyhood. Now people were dancing to jazz rhythms—the fox-trot, the one-step, the two-step, and, later on, Latin American dances like the tango and the rumba. The music they sang and danced to, and soon were hearing on the radio, reflected their new freedom and a more easygoing attitude toward life in general. And that music was in George's blood. He had heard it as a very young man in the nightclubs of Harlem. To him it was neither white nor black. He had heard that the blues had begun with the spirituals black people sang, but spirituals themselves apparently were a combination of white revival camp songs with African tunes and rhythms. Whatever its origins, to George all this was *American* music, and it was all wonderful. He listened hard, especially to the blues, and studied the so-called blue notes peculiar to jazz with the same fervor he brought to a concert of classical music, or to his studies in harmony with Edward Kilenyi. For if George was in some ways ahead of his time, in other ways he was very much a part of it.

Around this period, another George—George White—asked Gershwin to come and visit him in Detroit to talk about writing the score for one of his elaborate musical revues, which were known as *George White's Scandals*. The *Scandals* had started in competition with the big spectacles known as the *Ziegfeld Follies*, produced by White's rival, Florenz Ziegfeld: glittering shows presenting lots of leggy girls in tall headdresses and fancy costumes, comedy skits, and lavish production numbers. For a while, George worked for Florenz Ziegfeld as the rehearsal pianist for his show, the *Ziegfeld Follies of 1918*. After meeting with White and signing a contract, George came home to New York to write six numbers for the 1920 edition of the *Scandals* with lyricist Arthur Jackson.

The show opened at the Globe Theater on June 1, 1920, and could safely be called a success. It ran for 318 performances.

Two years later, for the 1922 *Scandals*, George tried something that would have been unthinkable for most Broadway composers. He decided to write a one-act jazz opera that would be presented as part of the show. The summer before, he had enrolled in courses in the music department at Columbia University. He had also been getting up early—for show business people like George, 8:30 in the morning is generally regarded as the middle of the night—to study orchestration. At this point he had begun to feel hemmed in by the boundaries of popular music and wanted to test his talents against something more challenging.

George sat down to compose an opera for an all-black cast that would be set in Harlem in "a basement cafe near 135th Street and Lenox Avenue." The story was simple, probably too simple. A gambler named Joe is in love with a girl named Vi. An entertainer in the same cafe, Tom, also has his eyes on Vi. When Joe gets a letter from his mother in Georgia and decides to go home to pay her a visit, Tom tells Vi that Joe is really visiting another woman. When Joe comes back, in a jealous rage Vi shoots him dead.

Despite its silly plot, *Blue Monday Blues* contains some wonderful music that could only be by George Gershwin. In more ways than one, the opera anticipated the music of *Porgy and Bess*. But the tired businessmen who spent their money to be entertained at *George White's Scandals* didn't care for it, not at all. After one performance the opera was cut out of the *Scandals*. But a stout bandleader with a round face and a tiny mustache named Paul Whiteman had seen it, and he considered the music remarkable. Unfortunately, the critics didn't feel the same way. One critic in the *New York World* called it "the most dismal, stupid, and incredible blackface sketch that has probably ever been perpetrated. In it a dusky soprano finally killed her gambling man. She should have shot all her associates the moment they appeared and then turned the pistol on herself." Many people counseled George to stick to popular stuff. George used to say that as a result of what he had gone through with *Blue Monday Blues,* or *Blue Monday,* as it came to be known, he developed what he called composer's stomach, a kind of indigestion that plagued him for the rest of his life, although no doctor he consulted ever put a medical label on it.

That same year, 1922, there were two Gershwin songs in other Broadway shows. One was "Do It Again," sung by the extremely talented and popular performer Irene Bordoni in *The French Doll.* The other partially brought true a dream of George's youth, to write music for his good friends Fred and Adele Astaire, who sang his song "Tra-La-La" in a musical called *For Goodness Sake.*

At all the right parties in town those days there would be George Gershwin at the piano playing his own songs. He liked nothing better than to sit at the keyboard, one of the cigars he had taken to smoking clamped firmly in his jaw, playing tunes and ingenious variations on those tunes, as admirers surrounded him and hung on his every note. George, who never suffered from shyness or a lack of confidence in himself, once explained that somehow, when he didn't play the piano at a party, he wound up not really having a good time.

As a composer, too, George was in demand everywhere. "Swanee" had crossed the ocean to England, and George himself was offered a round-trip boat ticket plus $1,500 to go to England and compose the songs for a London revue.

Writing to Ira as "Dear Iz," the name they still called him at home, George reported, "Well, ol boy, here I am in London almost 24 hours, or rather only 24 hours & the rain is coming down in the manner we've heard about for years." That rain may well have been the inspiration for the haunting song he later wrote with Ira, "A Foggy Day."

A real thrill for George, as he wrote in that same letter, was when he handed over his passport after the boat landed in Southampton and the man who stamped it looked up and asked, "Writer of 'Swanee'?" "Couldn't ask," George wrote with his usual frankness about his own vanity, "for a more pleasant entrance into a country." In London, George later found himself a real celebrity, being asked for interviews by newspaper reporters and even invited to compose a ragtime opera. Unfortunately, the songs he wrote for what was finally

A typical pose—George playing the piano and singing

called *The Rainbow* turned out to be not quite top drawer, and the show soon folded. When he left to go home, the only Gershwin song still being sung in England was "Swanee."

Meanwhile, jazz was more and more taking the center stage of American music. Not only black musicians but even all-white groups like the Original Dixieland Jazz Band were

Eva Gauthier

packing in audiences for this all-American sound. Pretty soon
the highbrows were taking it seriously, and ministers were
denouncing it from the pulpit. All the evils of the day, from
alcoholism to suicide, were blamed on jazz.

One place that seemed safe from this new music was the
concert hall—until one night when a French singer named
Eva Gauthier gave a "Recital of Ancient and Modern Music

for Voice" at Aeolian Hall, where only classical music had ever been played, and always for the most serious audiences. On the evening of November 1, 1923, Mme. Gauthier, appearing in a long-sleeved black velvet evening gown and huge diamond earrings, offered songs old and new from a variety of times and places. They included such twentieth-century masters of classical music as Béla Bartók and Paul Hindemith, then songs by Irving Berlin, Jerome Kern, Walter Donaldson, and finally George Gershwin. That night, "I'll Build a Stairway to Paradise," which had been staged as an elaborate number replete with moving staircases in the 1922 edition of the *Scandals,* along with "Innocent Ingenue Baby" and, yes, "Swanee," were heard for the first time in a concert hall. It was as George always believed; the popular song of today might well become the art song of tomorrow. The line between the two was very thin and could be crossed.

The audience loved the concert, and so did the critics, in spite of what one of them, Deems Taylor, who later became a great champion of Gershwin's music, called its "vulgar moments." That evening also marked the first time George appeared on stage as a concert pianist playing his own music, crossing in still another way the seemingly uncrossable barrier between the worlds of jazz and Tin Pan Alley, and the world of serious music. It was the first such time for George. It was not to be the last.

After the Eva Gauthier concert, George found himself moving more and more in a world of celebrities and fashionable homes. There were glamorous parties on Park Avenue and Fifth Avenue among the social elite. People recall him at those parties as lacking in polish at first, having to be reminded to take the cigar out of his mouth when he was introduced to a young lady. But he learned fast. Soon he was at home not only with the movie stars of the day—Mary Pickford, Douglas Fairbanks, Sr., Maurice Chevalier, Gertrude Lawrence—but with the society people, too.

10

An American Rhapsody

There were always several things happening at once in George's life as a composer. Even as Eva Gauthier was bringing his songs to Aeolian Hall, he was involved with a musical called *Sweet Little Devil*. He was getting ready to go to Boston for a tryout when one night, while he and Ira were playing pool at a favorite hangout for songwriters on Broadway called the Ambassador Billiard Parlor, a small news item in the *New York Tribune* caught Ira's eye: "Whiteman Judges Named . . . Committee Will Decide 'What Is American Music.' "

The item went on to announce that Paul Whiteman, the bandleader, would give a concert to be called "An Experiment in Modern Music," at which judges would pass on what American music was. The panel of judges included such exalted names in the musical world as the composer Sergei Rachmaninoff, the violinists Jascha Heifetz and Efrem Zimbalist, and the opera singer Alma Gluck.

The article went on to state that Irving Berlin was writing

a "syncopated tone poem" for the occasion, that Victor Herbert was preparing a suite of serenades, and that "George Gershwin is at work on a jazz concerto. . . ." George remembered that Whiteman, who was deeply interested in the future of American music, had talked to him about a jazz concerto. Whiteman had never forgotten the music of *Blue Monday*, which was such a failure in the 1922 *Scandals*. But nobody had told George he was writing a piano concerto for this Whiteman concert. He called Whiteman to ask if what Ira had read in the paper was true. It was. But the date of that phone call was January 4, 1924. *Sweet Little Devil* was about to open in New York on the 21st. The Whiteman concert was set for Lincoln's birthday, February 12. Even to a fast worker like George, the idea of composing an entire piano concerto in such a brief space of time seemed clearly impossible.

But the seed had been planted in his busy mind. By the time George boarded the train to Boston for the *Sweet Little Devil* tryout, ideas had begun to sprout. Then a curious thing happened. As the train sped toward Boston, George could hear music in the very clicking of the wheels. (He once said he could hear music "in the heart of noise.") Soon he thought of calling the music taking shape in his head an *American Rhapsody*. When he returned, the general outlines of his rhapsody were already clear in his imagination. He knew, for example, that Ross Gorman, the clarinetist in Paul Whiteman's orchestra, was able to play an especially difficult musical run right up the scale on his clarinet (a *glissando* is the technical term for it.) George decided that his rhapsody ought to open that way. Each day new ideas for the piece crowded his thoughts. By January 7 he was hard at work on the final draft, composing the passages on an old upright piano in the back room of the apartment on 110th Street where the Gershwin clan happened to be living at the time.

In addition to George and his parents, Arthur and Frankie were living in that apartment too, and there was a constant stream of visitors. But George would close the door to the room, light a cigar, sit down at the upright, and compose away.

Although he had taken a course in orchestration at Columbia and had been continuing his musical studies the year before under a composer named Rubin Goldmark, George still didn't know much about how to score music for various instruments. He wrote his rhapsody for two pianos, with indications here and there as to what parts other instruments should play. From these pages Ferde Grofé, a young composer and Paul Whiteman's orchestrator and arranger, set to work getting the music ready for the February concert. Grofé turned to jazz for the effects he wanted: moaning saxophones, a muted trumpet (with a hat like a derby over the bell to create a certain kind of sound), and the homely strumming of instruments not usually heard in classical music, such as the banjo. While he worked, Grofé spent many an hour at the Gershwin apartment, drinking cups of tea that Rose was happy to brew for him and chatting away with Pop Gershwin. It was Ira who came up with the title *Rhapsody in Blue*, which sounded right for a jazz concert. By February 4, three weeks after George set down the first notes of his piece, the orchestration was finished.

Rehearsals started at the Palais Royal, a nightclub on 48th Street where the Whiteman band was appearing in the evenings. There in the empty club, after hours, with chairs stacked up on tables, the air still heavy with cigarette smoke, the lights dim, George's *Rhapsody in Blue* took shape over five difficult days of rehearsal.

The fact is, George never thought of his first big serious piece, or any of those that followed, as symphonic jazz, which is what many writers came to call it. To him, it was simply a work for jazz band and piano.

And what a work it is! From the first note of that climbing wail on the clarinet, teetering like a circus acrobat balancing his way as he climbs up a high wire, this is music that seems to find its song in the tenements and teeming streets, the chants in the little synagogues on the Lower East Side, the folk tunes from Eastern Europe George heard in his childhood, even the tunes he plugged in Tin Pan Alley.

And yet, too, this is music that belongs to the stage. It moves fast like a tricky dance routine in a vaudeville show, glittering like dancers in showy costumes as one after another of the instruments strut their stuff. But listen to the piano. How nervous it is, how high strung, how restless and eager to get on with things. Yes, that's George all right, that's the song of the city boy, maybe the song of the city itself! Then comes the second section, sometimes with just a few instruments and the piano, sometimes the piano alone, and here the music reels. Then all of a sudden the whole mood shifts again, the lights seem to go down, everything becomes suddenly sad, and a mournful melody announces the third section of the rhapsody. This blues theme seems to express the lonely side of being alive. To be sure, it is also a jazzy blues, a blues borrowed in mood from the black South, and at the same time a strangely Jewish blues. This blues sings its sorrowful song, and all the longing and emptiness beneath the glitter of the whole jazz age might be mirrored in this mournful music. Then, just when it seems impossible for that bluest of blues to hold back its tears an instant longer, the whole mood suddenly changes again. George's *Rhapsody in Blue* shakes off its blues, sheds its dark mood, stops feeling sorry for itself, and dances joyfully to a blaring all-American stage-show finish.

On the snowy night of February 12, 1924, when the *Rhapsody* was heard at an overlong and sometimes boring concert, it was the twenty-second of twenty-three numbers, mostly by American composers.

When the time came for George's piece, his composer's stomach was really acting up. The orchestra was playing Rudolf Friml's "Donkey Serenade," submitted for the concert under the French title "Chansonette" (which means little song). George paced up and down in the wings, worrying about going out in front of an audience to play a work that he and Ferde Grofé hadn't even had time to score completely. Some of the most famous people in the musical world of New York were out there. What if he fell flat on his face, made a fool of himself? Then George went out and, the only expression for it is "faced the music."

It had cost Whiteman so much to put on his "Experiment in Modern Music," what with its fancy printed program and long hours of rehearsal, that he lost $7,000. Yet even with additional members added to his orchestra, there were only twenty-three of them to play the thirty-six instruments called for in Ferde Grofé's orchestration. Some of the players had to put down one instrument and snatch up another to keep pace with the music. Many pages hadn't been finished and contained instructions for the conductor to wait for a nod from the pianist before bringing in the orchestra. George was such a skilled performer by then that he was able to improvise the missing passages.

How did the world receive George Gershwin's *Rhapsody*? By the time the long program reached that piece the audience was practically asleep, but the wild whoop on the clarinet woke them up again. The applause that greeted the performance was long and loud. Pop Gershwin, who always timed his son's works and judged them by their length, was pleased to see that the *Rhapsody* had clocked in at more than fifteen minutes.

The critics didn't agree about the *Rhapsody*. They never would about any of George's serious compositions during his lifetime, or even since. One actually spoke of the "lifelessness of its melody and harmony" and called the whole thing "stagey," although he did have a few kind words to say about Mr. Grofé's colorful orchestration. Another, Olin Downes in the *New York Times*, wrote of the "extraordinary

The Paul Whiteman Band at Aeolian Hall to introduce *Rhapsody in Blue*, 1924

talent" of the composer. An admirer of George's music named Carl Van Vechten declared the *Rhapsody* "the foremost serious effort by an American composer."

Rhapsody in Blue has survived just about everything that has been written of it, and continues to this day to be a favorite in the concert halls of the entire civilized world.

As for George, when the newspaper reviews came out, he didn't have time to think much about them one way or another. He was polishing up new songs for the 1924 edition of the *Scandals* and getting ready to go to England again to write another score for a new musical called *Primrose*.

11

A Time for Play

What did George do when he wasn't working, or studying music, or pursuing his ambitions as a composer? Some who knew him got the impression that he was always working, but that wasn't quite true.

He loved to go to the theater and saw as many musicals as he could. Since 1918, when he and his friend and collaborating lyricist Irving Caesar met at Remick's and started going to Jerome Kern musicals together, George had always found the world of the stage a place of enchantment.

George loved games. When he discovered golf he played the game every minute that he could find for it and talked about it all the time. Other enthusiasms that he took up included backgammon, croquet, Ping-Pong, billiards, photography, swimming, fishing, word games, and roulette. Some of these hobbies he abandoned as abruptly as he had acquired them.

He kept himself in shape with calisthenics. He was a good athlete and a good dancer, too, often entertaining his friends

Above and right: George pursues other interests

with an accurate imitation of Fred Astaire or some other celebrated dancer he had met.

George always made friends easily. In 1915, while he was holding down the job at Remick's, Ira had introduced him to Lou and Herman Paley, brothers who lived not far from the Gershwins, and George had made their apartment one in a series of his homes away from home. Lou was an English teacher who also wrote song lyrics. Eventually, George set a number of those lyrics to music; somehow he always seemed

to wind up combining business with pleasure! Herman Paley was a songwriter who, like George, had studied under Charles Hambitzer. When the Paleys moved to Greenwich Village, their new apartment became a second home for George.

After Lou Paley married Emily Strunsky, George spent much of his spare time with both of them. George often commented that Emily was the sort of woman he would like to marry. Sunday evenings at their home he met other young musicians, painters, writers, and people interested in the arts. There would be talk about books and the theater, at which Ira, often present, expressed his opinions more frequently than George, and when the serious part of the evening was over, there were games of charades. Sometimes the discussions got pretty heated, especially about such matters as modern music. Some of the Paleys' friends, who refused to believe jazz could ever really be part of serious music, wondered privately why in the world the Paleys bothered with a ragtime piano player like George, and would ask the Paleys so when the Gershwin brothers weren't around. The Paleys would reply simply that they considered George a genius.

It was through the Paleys that Ira met Emily's attractive sister Leonore Strunsky, who in the mid 1920s became his wife. The Paleys also introduced George to their niece Mabel Pleshette, who, he discovered, had been still another Hambitzer student. When Mabel married Robert Schirmer, a member of the famed Schirmer family of music publishers, another lifelong friend was added to George's ever-growing list.

Yet another friend George made at the Paleys' was Lou's cousin George Pallay. He was a stockbroker about two years younger than Gershwin. They met in 1918, and the two Georges would spend many an evening making the rounds of the nightclubs, usually with especially good-looking chorus girls. Pallay was one of the few who became somebody George could confide in about his personal problems.

From the time he was in his teens, George had many girlfriends. He was the kind of young man who used to be called
a stage-door Johnny, turning up at the stage door with a
bouquet of flowers and waiting to take some long-legged
chorus girl out to dinner. He knew many beautiful young
women, but somehow things never got serious enough to
lead to marriage, and in the presence of women George never
got over a certain youthful shyness and awkwardness. Besides, music always came first. Once at a party he had a
stunning young woman on his lap. When somebody asked
him to play the piano, he got up so fast she fell on the floor.
Only toward the end of his life, when he fell in love with
the movie star Paulette Goddard, did he really intend to
marry. In her case, that might have been especially complicated, since she was believed to be already secretly married
to Charlie Chaplin. Nobody ever did find out whether she
and Chaplin were legally married, though they lived together
as husband and wife.

And so, although there were many women in George's
life, except for Paulette Goddard—who came into that life
toward the end of it—there was never the "one woman" he
kept hoping to meet and marry. In 1918 he fell in love with
a schoolteacher; in 1919 it was a young woman who played
the piano. A year later the love of his life was a showgirl
in the Ziegfeld Follies. There was more than one chorus girl.
Then there was an educated young woman who left him to
marry an economist in Albania. A movie actress named Aileen
Pringle caught his fancy for a while. He used to refer to her
as the "intellectual aristocrat of the screen," and she was also
rather beautiful. There were actresses, and society women,
and the French movie star Simone Simon, who was rumored
to have given him a gold key to her estate in West Los Angeles. Why didn't he marry one of them? One of the chorus
girls played some of his music on the piano, and he couldn't
stand the way she played. Another woman was too old for
him, he decided. Still another was too upper class; he felt

uneasy about the social world she moved in. "I'm a guy," he said, "that will always have the touch of the tenement in me." The sort of woman he thought might be right for him was always already married to somebody else.

In the presence of women, even when he was world famous, George was not only often rather shy and self-conscious, but in some ways something of a prude—as was Ira. His sister Frankie remembers they were always telling her she was wearing too much makeup, and to pull her skirts down, when she was a teenager. He was always afraid he might be rejected by a beautiful woman. He didn't lavish gifts on his girlfriends for fear they might think he was trying to buy their affection. The women he saw were mostly those who sought him out rather than the other way around. Once, a young woman, bored at a party somewhere in a building where he lived, came up to see him because she'd heard he lived there. When George was sharing a house with Ira and his wife, there was another woman who, pretending she was visiting the Ira Gershwins, would slip over to George's by way of a connecting terrace. One time he heard that a woman he was particularly fond of had just married somebody else. He told Ira, "I'd be terribly heartbroken if I weren't so damned busy."

Kitty Carlisle, the actress who later became the wife of playwright Moss Hart, recalls going out with George and being thrilled when he told her he had written a waltz just for her. Later she found out that the line containing her name could be changed to substitute the name of any young woman George was trying to impress at the moment—not the kindest of pranks, but one that seemed always to take in the latest victim.

One woman George especially admired was Kay Swift. A composer of popular songs, she wrote a number of hits and the entire score of the musicals *Fine and Dandy* and *The Little Show*. She was the wife of the financier James Warburg; they

Kay Swift

were later divorced. Warburg also wrote lyrics for songs, under the name of Paul James.

Kay was brilliant. She had studied music in a serious way. She was a sophisticated woman with much personal charm.

George first met her and her husband one evening in 1925 when a cellist he knew brought him to their home. George played the piano for hours, then sprang up and said he had to leave for England that very evening. The friendship between George and Kay continued and became a close one personally and professionally. She regarded him as a genius and was often with him when he was working on his music. She helped him edit his manuscripts. He always heeded her shrewd criticism. They would play two-piano arrangements together, not only of his works but also of the classics. She would fill his apartment with flowers. If George came close to really falling in love with anybody, it was certainly with Kay Swift.

At the Warburgs' farm in Connecticut, which he visited often, George learned how to ride a horse. He called it horse riding. When Kay corrected him, explaining that the proper term was horseback riding, he promised to say it right but soon went right back to calling it horse riding again. Kay also taught George far more than how to ride a horse. Thanks to her, his cultural interests began to extend beyond music, especially to painting.

In her eighties, Kay Swift was still an alert and handsome woman who vividly remembered the years of her friendship with George. Whether it had ever developed into a love affair, she refused to say. The thing she remembered best about George was how no matter whether it was work or play, he put every ounce of himself into whatever he was doing. "He was a marvelous friend," she said, "terrific. Once, when I gave a lecture on modern culture, I looked around the audience, and there he was! He was genuinely interested in people. And he encouraged people, especially if they had talent."

After George died, Kay Swift helped to find and put in order many songs and ideas for music he had worked on when she was with him, and then put aside.

Carl Van Vechten, a music critic and photographer who later devoted himself to writing novels, was one of the first influential figures in the world of the performing arts to champion George's talent and predict a great future for him.

In his autobiography, *Passport to Paris*, the composer of "April in Paris," Vernon Duke, refers often to the role George Gershwin played in helping him along in his career as well as in his complicated personal life. He tells of George's "customary generosity and big-brother kindness" when he needed him. For George, although regarded by many as self-centered and self-admiring, frequently went out of his way to lend a helping hand to friends and members of his family.

Oscar Levant, the pianist, composer, pundit, house clown, and movie actor, had been twelve when he first saw George at the piano with the band at a performance of a musical in Pittsburgh. At sixteen Levant had left Pittsburgh for New York. He was the pianist in a band run by the popular maestro Ben Bernie when a songwriter named Phil Charig introduced him to George. This was the beginning of a love-hate relationship that went on for many years. Indeed, in 1925 Levant did a recording on the Brunswick label of *Rhapsody in Blue*. He was also the pianist in other important recordings of George's works. Levant is the source of many amusing tales about George and his family. Once they were traveling by train to Pittsburgh on a concert tour, with Oscar about to make his debut at last as a pianist in his own hometown. Oscar lay sleepless in an upper berth, George below him in a lower. Apparently Oscar's reading light was keeping George awake. George opened one eye and murmured drowsily, "Upper berth, lower berth. That's the difference between talent and genius." Oscar got his revenge at a party where George, as usual, was entertaining at the piano. A knot of people were gathered around the composer, offering admiring remarks about his music, his piano playing, and his skill as an artist and in leading an orchestra. During a rare pause, Oscar asked his famous question: "George, if you had it all to do over, would you still fall in love with yourself?"

There were hundreds of others who knew George, and as his fame increased there would be hundreds more, for by the midtwenties everybody wanted to know him. Nothing succeeds like success. Yet those who knew him best say that the smiling, handsome young man surrounded by friends and acquaintances at parties was really a very lonely young man. They say perhaps he sought in his music a way to fill a kind of emptiness in his life that even falling in love with beautiful women never seemed to fill.

Perhaps George's closest friend was a wirehaired terrier named Tony who was always running away and was once kidnapped, making newspaper headlines, but always managed to find his way back to his master.

12

Making Every Minute Count

Unlike the last show George had worked on in London, *Primrose* was a smash hit. As usual he had no time to bask for long in the praise of the critics or to hang around London. He had to rush back to New York, where Alex Aarons and his partner, Vinton Freedley, wanted him to write the songs for a big new musical they were producing, to be called *Lady, Be Good!*

By now, George was leading a double life, one foot in the popular music world, the other in concert music. Walter Damrosch, the conductor of the New York Symphony Orchestra (today the New York Philharmonic), had heard *Rhapsody in Blue* at Aeolian Hall. He was always encouraging American composers, and had already invited George to write a piano concerto that would have its premiere not in Aeolian Hall but in a place with an even more respectable reputation, Carnegie Hall itself.

At that time, George was also the hottest thing on Broadway. He was busy writing the music for no fewer than four

With Alex Aarons, 1926

Broadway shows—*Tip-Toes*; *Song of the Flame*; *Lady, Be Good!*
and *Tell Me No More*. Then he and his brother Ira holed up
with another lyricist who frequently worked with George,
Buddy DeSylva, to write some of their best songs for *Lady,
Be Good!* most memorably the tricky number called "Fascinating Rhythm." Among the performers in *Lady, Be Good!*
were George's old friends Fred and Adele Astaire. Indeed,

it was *Lady, Be Good!* when it opened in December 1924, that made them stars.

That same year, George, Ira, and Buddy DeSylva were off to London once more to supply the songs for *Tell Me More.* It is interesting that the original title was supposed to be *My Fair Lady*, a fact that Frederick Loewe and Alan Jay Lerner happened to recall many years later when they decided to set George Bernard Shaw's play, *Pygmalion*, to music.

It was while in London working on *Tell Me More* that George first started sketching ideas for his piano concerto.

He had bought a book about concertos to help him figure out how to write one. He also read another book, a volume on orchestration, because he was determined to orchestrate the work himself. He had already orchestrated some of his own songs for *Primrose*.

In all, the years 1924 and 1925 found George busier than ever. Not that Ira was idle. Ira had also been writing lyrics for composer Vincent Youmans and others. And it was only when he wrote the words for the songs in *Be Yourself*, a show with music by Lewis Gensler and Milton Schwarzwald as well as George, that Ira came out from behind the made-up name Arthur Francis and began to use his own. From then on, when the brothers collaborated, it would be as George and Ira Gershwin.

In a profile of George written for the *New Yorker* magazine in 1929, the playwright S. N. Behrman told of visiting George in the living room of the Gershwin apartment on 110th Street, "working on the score of the *Concerto in F* in a room in which there must have been six other people talking among themselves, having tea, and playing checkers. In those days," Behrman wrote, "George used to mumble ineffectually that what he needed was some privacy." Finally the family decided to move to a five-story house on West 103rd Street.

A visitor might encounter several people from the neighborhood having a game of pool on the first floor, Arthur

The Gershwins' home on West 103rd Street

Gershwin up on the third floor, and Ira and his wife, Leonore, on the fourth.

On the top floor was George's study. The walls were covered with inscribed photographs of famous people. His books and music and the mementos of his career were there. And it was there, despite the buzz of conversation from the floors below, that George did his work. He would often start late at night and work until dawn. He would sit at his Steinway piano, bare to the waist, puffing on one of his cigars, working out the ideas that constantly went through his head. Once he lost a sketchbook with notes for some forty songs. He shrugged off the loss. He said he had too many other ideas to worry about it. But he worked hard turning the ideas he did have into actual music.

On that top floor, George also entertained visitors from all over the world, including world-famous musicians who came to praise his work. He would welcome both serious and popular composers who sought his help, and always tried to be of real help if he could. A high school student who came to interview him for his school paper was treated as seriously as the music editor of a major big-city newspaper. He answered every phone call. And when he wasn't out attending parties at the homes of rich and influential people, he held his own parties, playing the piano for hours to entertain his friends or talking shop with his colleagues.

When he was in London in 1925 for a reprise of the Eva Gauthier concert, George was a popular figure with the English public and even with royalty. He was honored by cousins of King George V, invited to Buckingham Palace by the Prince of Wales and to parties by the Duke of Kent, Prince George. In fact, on the wall of the New York house hung a photograph of the duke inscribed "From George to George."

Eventually, claiming he needed his privacy to compose, George rented a room a few blocks away from the Gershwin townhouse at the Whitehall Hotel, so he could work on the songs for still another musical slated for Broadway called *Funny Face*. But George, for all his talk of needing to be alone to work, really hated privacy and was almost always surrounded by people.

His friends caught up with him, even at the Whitehall. Finally one of George's countless friends, Ernest Hutcheson, a piano teacher, found George a little studio at a music colony where Hutcheson was teaching up in Chautauqua, New York. There George could work in peace and quiet, at least until four every afternoon, when the students from Hutcheson's class would flock around the piano to hear George play. And he loved the attention.

As George involved himself in the techniques of composition, he continued to feel, as he always had and always would, that emotion was the most important ingredient of any piece of music that bore his name. His concerto would not be cold, calculated exercises. He poured his soul into his work, as he did into everything.

George knew what a concerto was; if he didn't he found out from his book: a piece for a soloist and an orchestra, divided into three sections called movements, and based on forms developed by Johann Sebastian Bach and his sons, and by Haydn, Mozart, and Beethoven. The concerto had a standard form, but with plenty of room in it for a composer to write music in the language of his own day and style. George knew a lot about music by then. He knew the classics; he loved to play Debussy's preludes on the piano; he studied the advanced experimental scores by his contemporaries, Igor Stravinsky, Arnold Schoenberg, Alban Berg, Darius Milháud, Arthur Honneger, and Sergey Prokofiev. Of Manuel de Falla's colorful Spanish works he once commented, typically, "He's a kind of Spanish Gershwin."

Cigar in his mouth at a jaunty angle, for five months George sat long hours at the piano, working on his concerto. He dated every movement: the first, July 1925; the second, August–September; the third, September. Back at his room in the Whitehall, in October and November he worked on the orchestration. Soon afterward, he did something only a successful composer with money to spare could hope to do: He hired an orchestra of sixty players to rehearse his concerto

The creation of the *Concerto in F*. George with Walter Damrosch, 1925

at the Globe Theater with himself at the piano and his friend
Bill Daly conducting. In this way, George could hear how it
sounded and make changes and improvements as they played
it.

On the afternoon of December 3, 1925, it was pouring
outside Carnegie Hall, but inside, the auditorium was packed.
There wasn't an empty seat in the house. All the major critics
were there to judge whether the composer of *Rhapsody in
Blue* had been a mere flash in the pan or really had something
important to say in music. On the program were works by
the Russian composer Aleksandr Glazunov and the Frenchman Henri Rabaud, but the big event, everybody knew,
would be the performance by the American George Gershwin

of his new work for piano and orchestra. When Walter Damrosch introduced the work, he called its composer "the prince who has taken Cinderella"—he meant jazz—"by the hand and openly proclaimed her as princess to the astonished world, no doubt to the fury of her envious sisters. . . . " Yet the *Concerto in F* called for no jazz instruments, no wailing saxophones, no banjos. It was strictly scored for standard symphonic instruments.

Listen carefully, and once again you can hear in it the essence of George's personality, George's soul, George's world. As he wrote in an article in the *New York Tribune* that appeared the Sunday before the premiere, "The first movement employs the Charleston rhythm. It is quick and pulsating, representing the young enthusiastic spirit of American life. . . . " It is American life all right, but more specifically it is once again city life—a jumpy, sleepless, high-strung, energetic New Yorker's life. It is music also that almost sounds like a promise to bring true the old American dream of a better life, out of poverty into comfort and even luxury, as it scurries and soars like an elevator whisking the listener up to some luxurious penthouse for a breathtaking view of the city below—which has always looked best from a distance. This first movement, like the city itself, is calculated to bowl the listener over, and it ends with a sassy roar. The second movement begins with a blues on a muted trumpet. It might be the yearning dream of some lovely young girl looking down from the fire escape of an airless tenement on a hot summer night, a kind of city Cinderella imagining a fairy tale adventure with a prince who will dance her away to his kingdom. But it is in the final movement that all the feverish bustle of the big town finally springs to life. Here we are once again in the New York of George's boyhood, with all the clatter and rumble of the urban scene. There are measures of music here that mind the business of other measures—"kibbitzing" it's called in Yiddish—and other measures that laugh out loud, for what would a Gershwin concerto be without a sense of humor? Then, bursting free from the chaos and confusion, the crash of a cymbal, and a dash for the ending—like a dash for a subway train just leaving the platform—to bring the whole work to a brash, quick close.

Once again it was George at the keyboard playing the ambitious piano part, a far more finished affair than his earlier *Rhapsody*. And once again the critics were divided. Some felt the work was choppy, that George had not really mastered the concerto form, even that it was dull. Others felt George might better have let himself go more and written a less formal work.

But there were those who realized the intuitive genius that made the concerto a remarkable piece not quite like anything composed before it. As Samuel Chotzinoff said in the *New York World*, "He alone actually expresses us." Gershwin, he wrote, was "the present, a man with the talent to take 'crude material' and turn it into music of a kind those who have studied the subject all their lives but did not have his kind of talent could not hope to imitate."

13

"My Place Is Here—
My Time Is Now"

"I am a man without traditions," George Gershwin once said. "My place is here—my time is now." Yet his music has outlived him.

For Pop Gershwin, there was no question that the *Concerto in F* was a more important piece than *Rhapsody in Blue*. He had timed it with a stopwatch, and it was almost twice as long! The Gershwins were tremendously proud of their son, who had once been known as the Dapper Dan of Tin Pan Alley, and who had now brought his music to Carnegie Hall.

The same month that the *Concerto in F* had its premiere in Carnegie Hall, the musical *Tip-Toes* opened on Broadway, sending audiences out humming such delightful tunes as "Sweet and Low-Down," "Looking for a Boy," and "That Certain Feeling." Then, on December 29, there was a revival of George's one-act opera *Blue Monday*, under a new title, *135th Street*, when Paul Whiteman, as he had long planned, brought it to Carnegie Hall. The opera was done without scenery this time. Once again it was something less than a success.

In 1926 George went to England to prepare the London version of *Lady, Be Good!* He and Ira added a new song for the Astaires, "I'd Rather Charleston." That frenzied dance, the Charleston, was just then at the height of its popularity. While attending the tryouts of the show in Liverpool and with time to spare before the London opening, George decided to take a trip to Paris to spend a week with his friends Bob and Mabel Schirmer. He already thought of writing something that later became part of his next serious composition, *An American in Paris.* He jotted down the theme in a notebook and set it aside.

That same year, another Gershwin musical, *Oh, Kay!* starred the much-loved Gertrude Lawrence, who sang the best song in it, "Someone to Watch over Me." It ran for 156 performances at New York's Imperial Theater. That year Gershwin also introduced his five preludes for piano at a recital in New York. Three of them were later published and are still played often; the two remaining ones were only recently recorded for the first time by Michael Tilson Thomas.

At one point George and Ira, along with Ira's wife, took a house on forty acres in the country at Chumleigh Farm near Ossining, New York, to work on the songs—some of their best—for *Funny Face* and another musical they were doing, *Strike Up the Band.* When he wasn't working on lyrics, Ira spent hours painting. Also, Ira bought a secondhand Mercedes and all three Gershwins took driving lessons. Once he got his license, though, Ira never sat behind the wheel of a car again. The brothers also rode horses.

In 1927 the Astaires starred in *Funny Face,* which gave the world the charming song "S'Wonderful" and some of Ira's cleverest lyrics in "The Babbit and the Bromide." *Funny Face* chalked up 244 performances.

Broadway was coming to expect new hit songs every year from the pen of George Gershwin. But George decided that he needed some time away from the world of musical comedy. He felt he ought to travel, study some more, and maybe think seriously about writing an opera.

In the spring of 1928, four Gershwins—George; Ira; his wife, Leonore; and Frankie—went to Europe on a vacation trip that took them through England, France, and Germany. George even thought of looking up the great Nadia Boulanger when he got to Paris and studying under her. She had taught such outstanding American composers as Aaron Copland, Virgil Thomson, and Roy Harris. Ira's interests, as usual, were more literary. He wanted to see the Paris that was home to great American writers like Gertrude Stein, F. Scott Fitzgerald, and Ernest Hemingway.

George also had something else up his sleeve, a commission from the New York Symphony to write a new piece for orchestra. He was thinking of the theme he had jotted down when he had visited his friends the Schirmers in Paris two years before.

As it happened, before George went to Paris, Paris, one might say, came to George. In New York, Eva Gauthier, who had presented the concert where George Gershwin's music was first played in Aeolian Hall, had a special party for Maurice Ravel on March 7, 1928, for the French composer's fifty-third birthday. Ravel had just wound up a long tour of the United States and especially wanted to meet Gershwin. Although Ravel was the guest of honor that night, it was George who held the spotlight, playing the piano—mostly his own music, as usual—until dawn.

There is a fine story about that meeting, during which George is supposed to have asked Ravel if he would teach him orchestration, Ravel being one of the greatest orchestrators who ever lived. According to those who were there when George asked Ravel, through Mme. Gauthier, if he might become Ravel's pupil, the Frenchman's answer, as she translated it, was, "Why be a second-rate Ravel when you are already a first-rate Gershwin?" Ravel acknowledged that

April 1928, in Berlin

the two piano concertos he later composed were strongly influenced by the jazz he heard in America, and also especially by the music of Gershwin.

It was the end of March when the Gershwin foursome arrived in Paris. They were to stay three months and make side trips to other European cities. In Paris, George was once more the center of attention at a round of parties. He met a number of famous composers whose music he admired: Stravinsky, Poulenc, Prokofiev, Milhaud, Walton, and Ravel again. Vernon Duke was staying at the same hotel, the Majestic, and paid him a call. George played him a section of the sketch he was composing (any vacation with George was bound to be a working vacation) and Duke found part of it, according to a diary Ira was keeping at the time, "somewhat saccharine."

What Gershwin played for his visitors that day was the slow, "homesickness" blues from the piece about Paris on which he was working. He played it for everybody who came along, including the world-renowned conductor Leopold Stokowski. As for studying under Nadia Boulanger, she told George there was nothing she could teach him; he should just go on the way he was.

In Paris, the Gershwins discovered that performances were scheduled of both *Rhapsody in Blue* and the *Concerto in F*. George went to the performance of the *Rhapsody*, which was played by two pianists instead of one. He didn't like what he heard, but the audience did. So he stood up and took a bow anyhow. Wherever the Gershwins went in Paris, they were greeted with the famous slow theme from the *Rhapsody*. The same thing happened in Vienna. There was even a ballet performance of the *Rhapsody* in Paris by the Ballets Russes.

That trip to Paris might have taken Frankie Gershwin on an entirely different path in her life. One evening she and George went to a party at the home of their friend Mabel Schirmer. George, as always, was soon at the piano, but this

Paris, May 1928

Frankie Gershwin, 1920s

time, so was Frankie—singing his songs in a voice that has
been described as "small but true." Elsa Maxwell, who gave
some of the most famous parties in Europe, was there that
night and later reported to her friend Cole Porter what a
good singer Frances Gershwin was. As it happened, a revue
with songs by Porter was about to open at a nightclub called
Les Ambassadeurs. He invited Frankie to appear in the show

and sing a "Gershwin Specialty." She made a fine impression at the opening. According to Mabel Schirmer, "Frankie literally stopped the show." But George did not approve of his sister going back into show business, and neither did Ira. They were both always rather prudish, especially where their sister was concerned, and they talked her out of pursuing what might have been a spectacular career as a singer. When she was in her seventies, at last a record of her singing her brother's songs was released.

That summer, the Gershwins stopped off in London, where they attended the opening of a show for which Ira had written the lyrics, called *That's a Good Girl*. The music was by Phil Charig, the songwriter who had introduced Oscar Levant to George.

14

Taxi Horns
and Treasure Girls

The Gershwins returned to New York in June, and George immediately set about finishing the piano sketches for *An American in Paris*, which, for a while, he called a rhapsodic ballet. Then George started work on the orchestration, using not only the regular instruments of the symphony orchestra but also the funny-sounding taxi horns he had brought back from Paris. At the same time, he was collaborating with Ira on a new musical for Broadway, *Treasure Girl*. The star was the great Gertrude Lawrence, and two of the best Gershwin songs were in it: "I've Got a Crush on You" and "Feeling I'm Falling." But the show was not a hit.

On December 13, 1928, *An American in Paris* had its first performance in Carnegie Hall, just as had the *Concerto in F*.

Those who were with George that afternoon have described him as being in top form, tipping a shoeshine boy five dollars (a fortune in those days), and demonstrating a new dance step with a fine imitation of Fred Astaire.

An American in Paris is "program music"—it follows a kind

With the taxi horns bought in Paris for *An American in Paris*, 1929

of story line. According to George himself, the listener is to imagine that he is sauntering down the Champs-Élysées, one of the main boulevards of the French capital, on a mild spring morning. This he does to the first walking theme, taking in the sparkle and atmosphere of one of the world's most exciting and beautiful cities. He hears the old-fashioned taxi horns (the very ones George had imported for the performance). Having survived the wild Paris traffic, the American pauses before a café where from inside, he hears a bit of a popular piece of the moment called "La Maxixe." In his boyhood George had known this song as one that opens with the words "my mother gave me a nickel to buy a pickle." Then he resumes his walk to the tune of a second walking theme.

Our tourist goes on his way, crosses the river Seine, discovers the bohemian Left Bank, maybe meets a girl, maybe sits down at a sidewalk café for a quiet drink. Then all of a sudden, out of nowhere, he is overcome by a terrible bout of homesickness, expressed in the music by the kind of slow blues that is featured in nearly every one of the composer's big symphonic works. The books along the quay, the chestnut trees, the smiling sun—all the beauties and pleasures of the city suddenly mean nothing to him; he just wants to go home. As usual in a Gershwin piece, though, after the homesickness theme there comes an abrupt swing of mood. All at once the orchestra launches into a Charleston—a Charleston, to be sure, with a bit of a French accent. Perhaps the American has run into another American and they have decided to make a night of it on the town together, realizing that Paris is the most wonderful place in the entire world after all. The homesickness theme comes back briefly, but the music sweeps it away with a joyous finale, and the blues are forgotten.

"Merry, rollicking music," wrote one critic. "Nauseous claptrap," wrote another. But clearly, for those with the ears to hear it, George Gershwin's music was growing up, his mastery of the orchestra was greater than ever, and anybody with the wit to detect it could also enjoy all the humor written into those lively notes.

That very night in 1928, following the first performance of *An American in Paris*, there was a reception in George's honor in the home of friends who presented him with a huge brass humidor in which to store his cigars. Otto Kahn, a philanthropist and patron of the arts, made a speech during which— in an indirect way but plainly enough for anyone who could read between the lines—he invited George to compose a work for the Metropolitan Opera.

15

"A Motor That's Always Going"

"Deep down inside all the Gershwins—George, Ira, Frankie," their friend Mabel Schirmer once said, "there's a motor that's always going." (Arthur, though less driven, was also always occupied with music or some investment enterprise.) The thought of an opera was now very much on George's mind. Back in 1926 he had met DuBose Heyward, the author of a novel called *Porgy*, and his wife, Dorothy, in Atlantic City. *Porgy*, a story about the Gullah blacks of Charleston in an enclave called Catfish Row, was supposed to be produced on Broadway by the Theatre Guild; a year later it actually was. George had read the book and for several years had been thinking of basing an opera on it. Closer to his heart, though, at the time was the idea of writing an opera based on S. S. Ansky's Yiddish play *The Dybbuk*. It is a mystical tale about a young man who enters into the forbidden studies of the Kabbalah, the mystical branch of Judaism. He is punished by death and his soul enters the body of the woman he loves and has to be exorcised. George had already started to note down the melodies and rhythms of Hassidic dances, snatches of synagogue music, old Yiddish folk tunes. He wanted to go to Europe again and hear more of the Jewish music of Eastern Europe for himself. Alas, the rights to adapt Ansky's religious mystery play turned out not to be available, and George had to abandon the whole idea. At one point George thought of turning Eugene O'Neill's play *The Emperor Jones* into an opera.

George also thought for a while of writing an opera about "the melting pot of New York City itself, which is the symbolic and actual blend of the native and immigrant strains." In it he hoped to catch the musical essence of the many "clashing and blending" races and creeds that made up the city. His opera was to combine humor with tragedy, and be a product, as he wanted all his music to be, of "both head and heart."

Meanwhile, he turned his attention again to the lighter side of his art. When he was twenty he had been the rehearsal pianist for the super-showman Florenz Ziegfeld's *Ziegfeld Follies of 1918*. Early in 1928, several of his songs had been heard in Ziegfeld's show, *Rosalie*. Now he and Ira settled down to writing the songs for another Ziegfeld musical, to be called *Show Girl*. The star of that show was Al Jolson's wife, Ruby Keeler, who would soon become known to movie audiences everywhere as the dancer who makes good when the star of a Broadway musical breaks an ankle in the movie musical *42nd Street*.

In *Show Girl* the audience was also treated to a ballet set to the music of *An American in Paris* and there was a song, "Home Blues," based on the homesickness blues theme. But *Show Girl* proved to be a flop, and Ziegfeld blamed that on the Gershwins. He refused to pay them their royalties. They sued him, and then he sued them back for failing to write songs that would make his show a hit.

By then the Gershwin brothers were busy again, collaborating on the songs for still another musical, *Strike Up the*

Band. Once before, they had been involved with an earlier version of this musical based on a book by George S. Kaufman, the wittiest playwright of the period. But it had failed. Now a producer wanted to try again with a satirical fantasy about a war between Switzerland and the United States that starts when America tries to impose a 50 percent tax on Swiss cheese.

The playwright Morrie Ryskind had been brought in to fix up Kaufman's book, which the public had found too bitter in its humor, while the Gershwins set about revising the old songs and adding new ones. In the new version, the war against Switzerland took place in one of the character's dreams, and the cheese factory had been converted into a chocolate factory. This second time around, *Strike Up the Band* was a big success. One Gershwin song, and one of his best, that was supposed to be in *Strike Up the Band* was "The Man I Love." It had been dropped once, from *Lady, Be Good!* for slowing up the action, and had gone on to become a hit on its own in London after Lady Mountbatten, a friend and admirer of George's music, had taken the sheet music home with her after hearing it in New York. It had died during rehearsals of the first version of *Strike Up the Band*, and now it was dropped once more from the second. And yet, although it never found a home on Broadway, through the years that song has remained one of America's favorites.

Strike Up the Band was not the only Gershwin hit on the stage in 1930. With Ethel Merman and Ginger Rogers in the cast, *Girl Crazy* chalked up 272 performances, compared with 191 for *Strike Up the Band*. Some of the songs from that musical are still played: "Bidin' My Time," "But Not for Me," "Embraceable You," and "I Got Rhythm." When Ethel Merman, whose voice could be heard a block away, marched out and sang, "I got rhythm, I got music,/I got my man, Who could ask for anything more?" she really stopped the show.

Meanwhile, in February 1929, George's friend Nathaniel Shilkret recorded *An American in Paris* for RCA Victor. George,

George performing at Lewisohn Stadium

who can be heard playing a pianolike instrument called a celesta on that recording, got so enthusiastic during the rehearsal, that he had to be asked to leave, though he was back for the recording sessions. But George liked the records so much he used to practice conducting while playing them. In August of that year he embarked on still another career, conducting the piece for the first time at Lewisohn Stadium as well as playing the piano part in *Rhapsody in Blue*. He conducted it again in November 1929. And a month later, on Christmas Day, when *Strike Up the Band* opened, there he was, wearing what one critic described as the world's biggest white tie, along with a white gardenia, to conduct the orchestra. He hummed and sang along with the cast in what he once referred to as his "small but disagreeable voice." He certainly enjoyed himself. After that, he went off to Florida for a well-earned rest.

16

Pianos and Penthouses

For millions of Americans, the 1930s were a time of unemployment and serious hardship. For the Gershwins, it was a time of personal prosperity. George's boyhood dream of living in a penthouse had come true. Since 1928 he had been living in a penthouse apartment on West 75th Street and Riverside Drive with a sweeping view of the New York skyline to the south and the Hudson River and New Jersey beyond to the west. Actually, there were two penthouses—one for George and one for Ira and Leonore.

The apartments were connected by a terrace, making it easy for George and Ira to get together and collaborate. George's apartment was the last word in 1930s art deco modern. The furniture had angular lines; black-and-white decor and chrome fixtures made the place gleam like a set in a science-fiction movie of the period. Paintings George's cousin Henry Botkin had helped to collect decorated the walls.

George's bedroom at 33 Riverside Drive. The painted screen next to the bed is Henry Botkin's conception of *An American in Paris*

A few years later, George painted a self-portrait in evening clothes—white tie, tails, top hat—which he had modeled for by using several mirrors so that, in Oscar Levant's words, "the painting gave the illusion of four Gershwins instead of one."

George and Ira had always shown a talent for painting and drawing. Frankie is a fine painter. By the last few years of his life, George had so well mastered the medium that when his work was finally placed on exhibition, both art critics and the public took it seriously.

One of George's self-portraits

In one of the rooms stood the equipment George used to keep himself in shape, including a punching bag and a rowing machine. George usually wrote his music at night, often after coming from some party in town; Ira would fit words to the tune later.

Sometimes the idea for a new song would occur to George at a party while he was entertaining at the piano. In his own living room were two grand pianos, where he and Oscar

The fitness room

Levant occasionally tried out a composition before it was set for orchestra.

Levant has described penthouse life among the Gershwins in those days:

"Surrounding the two apartments (Ira had a fondness for singing George's settings of his lyrics) both from the pianos and the phonographs was a sporadic stream of talk embrac-

A corner of the Gershwin apartment, with shelves containing books, musical scores, and George's paintings above

ing prize fighting, music, painting, football. . . . The Gershwins' enthusiasm for Ping-Pong was communicated to me along with the scores, and we spent hours at the game. Amid this constant activity there was recurrently a recess for food, disguised as lunch, dinner, supper or midnight snack. . . . ''

Fortune seemed to be smiling on the Gershwins from every

George's Steinway baby grand

side. On the morning of November 2, 1930, their sister Frances married Leopold Godowsky, Jr. That afternoon, Mom and Pop Gershwin were off for a Florida holiday. Three days later George, Ira, and Leonore boarded a train for Hollywood. The Gershwin brothers had been invited there to supply the songs and music for a movie. For a few weeks' work, George would be paid $70,000, Ira $30,000.

In Beverly Hills, they rented a two-story Spanish-style villa that for a time had been home to Greta Garbo. "I am sleeping in the bed that she used," George liked to point out, adding that it hadn't helped his sleep any.

The Gershwins had been hired by the Fox Studio to work

on the music for a movie called *Delicious*, featuring two of the most popular stars of the period. Janet Gaynor and Charles Farrell. George was not a movie fan, and he said he was approaching his assignment with a humble attitude. Actually most of the songs he and Ira supplied for *Delicious* were leftovers from other scores, including a very funny routine called "Mischa, Yascha, Toscha, Sascha." But the movie, which was supposed to take place in New York City, also called for a dream sequence, for which George decided to compose a new rhapsody.

When he wasn't composing, George gave himself up to the outdoor life of Southern California. He went hiking with a trainer, played golf, and went swimming in Palm Springs. On New Year's Day the Gershwins drove to Caliente, Mexico, for a big party where two Spanish dancers performed to *Rhapsody in Blue*. In January 1931 they attended a concert by the Los Angeles Philharmonic where Artur Rodzinski, one of the great conductors of the day, included the local premiere of *An American in Paris*.

By the time the movie *Delicious* opened in 1931, there were only a few Gershwin songs and one minute of the new rhapsody still in it. One critic wrote, "George Gershwin is said to have written the music involved, but you'd never know it. Civilization hasn't had such a setback since the Dark Ages. . . . "

George decided to take the six-minute rhapsody he had composed for the movie and work it up into something more important. First he called it *Manhattan Rhapsody*, then *Rhapsody in Rivets*, and the opening theme does indeed suggest a city street in the throes of construction. Later he changed the name simply to *Second Rhapsody*. George worked long and hard on this music, with occasional suggestions from Ira, such as that he include a slow theme similar to the one that was so popular in *Rhapsody in Blue*.

The *Second Rhapsody* was not completed until late in May 1931, in New York. Arturo Toscanini was interested in con-

The *Delicious* team—Ira, George, and Guy Bolton

ducting the premiere of the new piece, but it was Serge Koussevitzky, in January 1932, who actually conducted the first performance with the Boston Symphony in Boston. The piece, incidentally, was dedicated to George's old friend and helper, Max Dreyfus.

In many ways, the *Second Rhapsody* is a work that goes deeper than the first and shows its composer to be a man who had grown up musically in several ways. Again it is a work of the city, a work rooted in George's Jewish temperament. Many passages express ideas developed as they had never been before by Gershwin. The piano is used throughout more as another instrument in the orchestra than as a solo instrument. In all, the colors of this rhapsody are deeper and darker, the tone more serious than in any of the long works that preceded it.

In the 1980s, the conductor Michael Tilson Thomas studied

the original score and recorded it the way he believed George would have wanted it to sound. Before that, arrangers were always tampering with the orchestration. In this new recording, the *Second Rhapsody* finally gets the serious respect it deserves.

George and Ira were beginning to turn to other things. One of their ideas was to use the form of musical comedy for political satire rather than just the usual boy-meets-girl, boy-loses-girl, boy-gets-girl formula that was the standard routine in those days. The idea appealed to George and appealed even more to Ira, who admired the comic operas of Gilbert and Sullivan, which had successfully made fun of British politics in the last years of the nineteenth century, and had everybody in England laughing except Queen Victoria. The Depression years made Americans more responsive to plays that laughed at the Establishment.

The musical that came to be called *Of Thee I Sing* really revolved around a simple joke: how John P. Wintergreen becomes president of the United States running on the platform of Love. The story also has to do with whether the woman he loves can bake corn muffins. *Of Thee I Sing* made Americans laugh out loud in the very depths of the Great Depression. And George, whose music could set the feet of audiences tapping in a concert hall, outdid himself this time. *Of Thee I Sing* contained the kind of music that had once belonged more in operas and operettas than in Broadway musicals. There were elaborate passages for chorus, complicated stretches for the orchestra. The songs were among the most winning the Gershwins had ever penned together: "Because, Because" and "Love Is Sweeping the Country," and the high-spirited "Who Cares?" A satire is a piece of writing that pokes fun at things, and *Of Thee I Sing* was a political satire that poked fun at American politics. The show ran for a staggering 441 performances, and on May 2, 1932, it was awarded the Pulitzer Prize in drama. Pop Gershwin's comment: "That Pulitzer must be a smart man." The music was not mentioned as part of the award, though it is the music—not the silly story written by two of Broadway's best writers, George S. Kaufman and Morrie Ryskind—that is still remembered.

Two weeks later, on May 15, 1932, Morris Gershwin died. This took the joy out of the Pulitzer Prize for Ira. It also changed George's plans for a trip to Europe. Instead, he decided to take a short vacation in Havana. But George could never just go on a trip and take it easy. It was no surprise to anybody who knew him that while he was in Cuba, George became interested in the lively music of that island and the instruments on which the Cubans played it. He brought home some of the instruments, along with an idea for a new symphony that would make use of them.

In July 1932, he set to work on a piece that later came to be known as his *Cuban Overture*. It is a stunning work, drenched in the atmosphere of the Caribbean island, making clever use of the sticks, bongos, gourds, and maracas George had brought back, reaching a climax in a wild rumba featuring those instruments backed by the full symphony orchestra. It is fun to hear, and demonstrates how much George had learned about the technical aspects of his craft. Its first performance was on August 15, 1932, at Lewisohn Stadium with the New York Philharmonic-Symphony Orchestra under Albert Coates, as part of an all-Gershwin program.

For that concert, George asked Oscar Levant to play the *Concerto in F*, since George himself was already scheduled to play both *Rhapsody in Blue* and the *Second Rhapsody*.

After the concert, according to Levant, well-wishers flocked around George to congratulate him on his music and on his playing. They shook his hand and said, "George, it was wonderful!"

If one is to believe Levant, what George said then was "That's all? Just wonderful?"

Meanwhile, Levant, an excellent pianist, stood around waiting for someone to make a comment about his playing of the concerto. Nobody came near him. Finally he went over to the group. "You could at least send one of them over to me," he told George. George's solution was to send over his brother Arthur. Later, though, he gave Levant a watch inscribed "From George to Oscar, Lewisohn Stadium, August 15, 1932." "It is by this watch," Levant wrote afterward, "that I have been late for every important appointment since then."

For the producers Alex Aarons and Vinton Freedley, who presented so many of the musicals on which the Gershwin brothers had worked, the Gershwins wrote still another score that year, for *Pardon My English*. But even though there were top-drawer Gershwin songs in it like "Isn't It a Pity?" and "The Lorelei," the show didn't last long. Neither did the next Gershwin musical, *Let 'Em Eat Cake*. Sequels are not often successful, and this was a sequel to *Of Thee I Sing* that brought back the character of John P. Wintergreen. He and his friends are defeated for reelection and decide to overthrow the government. The show had delightful songs in it, such as the lovely "Mine," but the story was weak and it just didn't go over. That made two flops in a row for the Gershwins.

George decided it was time to settle down to something serious, maybe write the opera based on DuBose Heyward's *Porgy* that he had been thinking about since 1926.

17

The Birth of Porgy

On March 29, 1932, when George was planning the trip to Europe he had to cancel because of his father's death, he had written to Heyward, "I am about to go abroad in a little over a week, and in thinking of ideas for new compositions, I came back to one that I had several years ago, namely *Porgy*, and the thought of setting it to music. It is still the most outstanding play I know about the colored people." Could Heyward possibly telephone him collect or maybe even meet him in Europe?

Heyward had answered right away, assuring George that the operatic rights to *Porgy* were "free and clear." But he was let down soon afterward when George wrote back to say that it would be almost a year before the music could be written because of his musical-comedy commitments.

There were other setbacks that almost killed the project. At one point Heyward heard from his agent that Al Jolson was planning to star in a musical based on *Porgy*, playing the role in blackface. Then came news that Jerome Kern and

Oscar Hammerstein II intended to write the score for a *Porgy* musical. Meanwhile, George, in the midst of moving from his modernistic penthouse apartment at 75th Street and Riverside Drive to a duplex on East 72nd Street, and busy working with Ira on new songs, had other things on his mind. *Porgy* was put aside until, on November 3, 1932, there was an item in the newspapers that brought the project unexpectedly back to life: Jolson, Kern, and Hammerstein had changed their minds about doing *Porgy*, given it up and let go all claims to the work.

A week later Dubose Heyward sent George "two copies of the first scene which I have worked over for you to start on."

George Gershwin was finally going to compose a full-length opera.

The story is really a simple one. It tells of a crippled beggar named Porgy who lives in a poor black neighborhood in Charleston, South Carolina, known as Catfish Row. Porgy falls in love with Bess, who is not the most proper woman in the world. She is unable to resist the strong and evil Crown, who pays attention to her when he feels like it and tosses her aside when he doesn't. She is also mixed up with a cynical drug peddler named Sportin' Life, who has lured her into becoming dependent on drugs. Porgy tries to make a good woman out of Bess. And when she comes home sick after an encounter with Crown during a picnic on nearby Kittiwah Island, Porgy, in a rage, kills Crown. But this does not make Bess his. She hangs around for a while; then Sportin' Life gets her back on the drug habit, and she goes off to Harlem with him. Porgy gets away with murdering Crown. But when he comes home to find Bess gone, not realizing how far it is to New York, he decides to go after her in a goat cart and bring her back. Curtain.

George's love of jazz, his early acquaintance with black musicians and their music, and his attempts to deal with a love story about black people in *Blue Monday*, all led him in the direction of *Porgy*. But even after writing to Heyward in 1932, George was sidetracked by the pressures of other projects. That year he was busy putting together *George Gershwin's Song Book*, piano versions of eighteen of his most famous songs—from "Swanee" to "Who Cares?" In 1933 there was the musical *Let 'Em Eat Cake*. He also wrote the ambitious work for piano and orchestra, *Variations on "I Got Rhythm"* in time for a 1934 tour. Then he started hosting his own radio programs. There were two series. The first was heard twice a week for fifteen minutes over the NBC network during the first half of 1934; the second was a weekly half-hour show broadcast coast to coast by CBS from September to the end of that year. On his programs, George interviewed fellow composers, played their songs as well as his own, and entertained guest celebrities from the world of musical theater.

After many letters between George and Heyward, in January 1934 George went off to travel with the tour. It lasted for twenty-eight busy days. When George got home he found a letter from Heyward reporting on several scenes he had written for the opera. It was really time for them to get together.

Following the tour, George started writing music for the first act. He sketched a little bit for this part of the opera, a little bit for that. "I am skipping around," he wrote. Soon Ira became involved in the project and was writing lyrics for it; up to then Heyward himself had written all the lyrics.

But Ira was writing the kinds of lyrics never heard in an opera before, words for songs like "A Woman Is a Sometime Thing," "It Ain't Necessarily So," "I Loves You, Porgy," "There's a Boat Dat's Leavin' Soon for New York," "A Red-Headed Woman," "Oh, I Can't Sit Down," and "Bess, You Is My Woman Now." Although George usually wrote his music first and then Ira supplied the words to fit, that happened only once here—for "I Got Plenty o' Nuttin'."

George said he wanted to hear "some real singing," the kind of black music on which he hoped to base much of what

George in Charleston, South Carolina, June 2, 1934, for a meeting with DuBose Heyward

he composed, and he got his wish. One day, during a trip to the marshland of South Carolina, outside a black church in a town called Hendersonville, George heard a complicated prayer sung by six voices. He later wrote a prayer of that

A relaxed moment on Folly Island—George with cousin Henry
Botkin, June 1934

kind for the big storm scene in the opera. On James Island,
not far from Folly Island, he also heard the "shouting" of
the Gullah blacks—which is what they called the complicated
rhythms they beat out with their hands and feet to accompany the singing of spirituals. One night George started
"shouting" with them and stole the show.

In June 1934, George, his art-expert cousin Harry Botkin,
and an assistant George had hired, Paul Mueller, moved into
a rented four-room cottage on Folly Island, a little island
about ten miles off the coast of Charleston. It was quite a
contrast to George's Manhattan duplex. Water had to be
brought in from Charleston, five gallons at a time. George
slept on an iron cot that was never made up. There was a
washbasin, an upright piano, and some hooks for clothes.
That was it.

At work on Folly Island

From the porch George could see the beach and the giant turtles that dozed in the sand, porpoises swimming in the sea, and the telltale fins of sharks. There were alligators, also, in swamps not too far off. All this was new to George, the city boy. He wrote to his mother, "The place down here looks like a battered, old South Sea Island. There was a storm two weeks ago which tore down a few houses along the beach and the place is so primitive they just let them stay that way. Imagine, there's not *one* telephone on the whole island." He added that he didn't think his comfort-loving mother would care too much for Folly Island, and advised her to stay home. Eventually the Heywards came over to the island. George was writing music as fast as he could get it down on the page. But seeing Harry Botkin painting, he couldn't resist taking time off to do some painting of his own.

George envied Henry not only the time he had to spare for painting but also his beard, and he decided that he would grow one, too. But he gave up after a couple of days. Still, deeply tanned, walking around bare-chested in a pair of white knickers and sandals, George on Folly Island did not look like the dapper fellow known to the world of show business on the island of Manhattan.

One day George called Dorothy Heyward back just as she was setting out on a trip to town. He invited her to come into the room where the piano was and "listen to the greatest music composed in America!" Such was the modesty of George Gershwin.

What George heard that summer—the shoutings, the prayers, the street cries of the women selling strawberries, the crabcake man and the man who sold honey—can all be heard in the music of *Porgy and Bess*, along with the beautiful six-part prayer based on the prayer he heard in Hendersonville. In August, George, his cousin, and Paul Mueller returned to New York. George went right on composing the opera.

In January 1935, George went down to stay at the home of his friend Emil Mosbacher in Palm Beach to orchestrate *Porgy and Bess*. When he had finished, there was a vocal score 560 pages long, and a score for orchestra running 700 pages. George signed the manuscript, and added "Finished August 23, 1935."

An opera on paper is one thing. To get a big, complex piece of work involving all the arts ready for actual performance on the stage is something else. But three days later, on August 26, rehearsals were actually under way.

To put on an opera is one of the most complicated undertakings imaginable. So many aspects of the performing arts are involved—the orchestra, singing, dancing, stage design, costumes, lighting, makeup—everything that has to do with music and with the theater all brought together in one big effort.

Putting the finishing touches on *Porgy and Bess,* 1935

Porgy and Bess was to be presented not on the stage of an opera house but on Broadway at the Alvin Theater, named for the two men who had produced so many musicals containing Gershwin's songs, Alex A. Aarons and Vinton Freedley. Rouben Mamoulian, who had directed *Porgy* on the stage, was called in to direct the opera. The cast, except for a few

The *Porgy and Bess* collaborators: George, DuBose Heyward, and Ira

minor characters, was made up entirely of black performers. George would not allow the opera to be sung by any cast but a black one. For the part of Porgy, a young man who taught music in Washington, D.C., Todd Duncan, was chosen. Bess was played by soprano Anne Brown. John W. Bubbles, famous up to then as half of the tap-dancing vaudeville team of Buck and Bubbles, was to be the wicked, scoffing Sportin' Life. Warren Coleman played the bully, Crown. The Eva Jessye Choir supplied the many difficult passages of choral music. Alexander Smallens, who had not long before conducted another all-black opera, Virgil Thomson's *Four Saints in Three Acts*, was brought in as conductor.

George's close friend Kay Swift, and a music editor, Dr. Albert Sirmay, who had worked on getting earlier Gershwin scores ready for publication, collaborated in preparing the opera score for the printers.

At first, during rehearsals, the performance was running longer than four hours. George, with his strong sense of the theater, agreed that cuts would have to be made. A section of piano music for the opening scene was eliminated. "The Buzzard Song," one of the most moving moments in the score, was cut. So was the trio in "Where Is My Bess?" There were countless other small cuts, so that by the time *Porgy and Bess* opened, it had come to resemble a musical comedy more and more and less and less the grand opera George had in mind. Instead of the recitatives—sung dialogue—linking one song or aria with the next and sustaining the musical flow, the dialogue was spoken most of the time. One passage after another was shortened. George had said he intended this to be a folk opera, and it kept getting folksier all the time.

Despite the eagerness of the public to see and hear *Porgy and Bess*, the critics turned up their noses on Tin Pan Alley's contender for acceptance as an operatic composer. As a matter of fact, the music critics liked it as a drama, and the drama critics liked the music, but most regarded it as a mixture of serious and popular styles that didn't really quite gel. Whatever George had set out to do, the verdict in 1935 was that he really hadn't done it.

The opera cost $70,000 to stage, and the entire investment was lost. Ira made about $2,000 out of the whole thing. Whatever money George made was spent on copying the parts for the singers and the orchestra.

Audiences and critics alike have since come to recognize the greatness of *Porgy and Bess*. Especially after all the cuts were restored and everything George had woven into his opera—the songs, the dances, the street cries, the brilliant orchestral passages that bring to life the whole atmosphere of Catfish Row—could finally be seen and heard as his genius had conceived it. Yet this kind of recognition did not come for *Porgy and Bess* until after George's death.

That opera is the sum total of everything George Gershwin

Porgy and Bess, 1935

had learned about music by the time he had reached the age
of thirty-seven. You can hear in it not only the jazz he came
to love in Harlem in his youth, the songs and chants of the
blacks whose music he heard and sang along with in Charleston, but even the music of the synagogue, which must somehow have gotten into his ears even though as a boy he was
seldom inside a Jewish house of worship. In the well-known
duet between Porgy and Bess, "Bess, You Is My Woman
Now," there is the line "Mornin' time an' evenin' time an'
summer time an' winter time. . . ." Not only are these words
right out of the Jewish prayer book (whether Ira realized
it or not when he wrote that line), but the music itself is al-

George takes a curtain call for *Porgy and Bess*, 1935

most exactly the same as what is sung in the synagogue.

Out of the music in his opera, Gershwin also wrote a five-movement suite for orchestra called *Catfish Row*, which was introduced by the Philadelphia Orchestra under Alexander Smallens at the Philadelphia Academy of Music on January 21, 1936. George had also written *Catfish Row* in the course of a much needed vacation in Mexico. While he was in Mexico, George looked for music that might inspire a Mexican-flavored composition, but failed to find any.

In 1935 George Gershwin also got some attention as a painter when a few of his canvasses were shown at a New York exhibition.

18

The Final Stop

The next stop for George and Ira was Hollywood, their second trip to the movie capital. The people at RKO studios who sent for them were a little worried about whether the team would be able to write a hit score for the next Fred Astaire–Ginger Rogers musical, which is what they had been invited to supply. Perhaps they were afraid that now that George had written an opera which in Hollywood was regarded as a flop, he would only want to write "highbrow" music instead of hits. Other studios had similar fears about George Gershwin. He put those fears to an end with a famous telegram to his Hollywood agent: "RUMORS ABOUT HIGHBROW MUSIC RIDICULOUS STOP AM OUT TO WRITE HITS."

And so in the summer of 1936, after a concert tour during which George played his own works on the piano and conducted his *Catfish Row* suite, George and Ira closed up their apartments on East 72nd Street, put their belongings in storage, and headed west.

Shortly before they left, George made his final public ap-

George and Ira board a plane in Newark, New Jersey, for their trip to California, August 1936

pearance in New York at a Lewisohn Stadium concert where he played *Rhapsody in Blue* and the *Concerto in F*, and the cast of *Porgy and Bess* sang selections from the opera.

In Los Angeles, the brothers were put up for a while at

The famous Gershwin brothers arrive in Los Angeles, California

the Beverly Wilshire Hotel where they wrote songs for a movie that was eventually known as *Shall We Dance*. Later they rented a big Spanish-style house in Beverly Hills. There they gave huge parties, which George photographed with

George with Mark Sandrich, the director for *Shall We Dance*

his home movie camera. To keep in California style, he sold his Buick and bought a Cord, the last word in automobile fashion that year. For *Shall We Dance* Ira and George wrote the songs "(I've Got) Beginner's Luck," "Slap That Bass," "Let's Call the Whole Thing Off," and "They Can't Take That Away from Me," all still popular half a century later. As a joke on the Hollywood custom of setting all movie music for huge orchestras, he also composed a piece called "Walking the Dog," deliberately scoring it for a small orchestra instead of a big one. That piece has since come to be known as "Promenade."

By that time, the Gershwin household also included Paul Mueller, who served as butler, houseman, and general as-

Left to right: Rudy Vallee, Irving Berlin, George, and Gene Buck of ASCAP

sistant to the composer, and Mrs. Mueller, who did most of the cooking.

George had attracted some new friends, including the world-famous composers Igor Stravinsky and Arnold Schoenberg, who also lived in Los Angeles. Inspired by Schoenberg, George was planning a string quartet and even thinking about writing a symphony.

He was seeing a lot of the movie star Paulette Goddard. He had known her when they were both growing up in New York. Now he had fallen in love with her and hoped she would leave Charlie Chaplin and marry him.

Yet he missed New York and his friends there, and was bored by what he described as the "phony glamour" of Hollywood.

George and Ira also learned, during the making of *Shall We Dance*, that once they turned in their songs, they would

George with Paulette Goddard

not be consulted very much about anything concerning the movie.

Soon afterward, in the spring of 1937, although George was tanned and looked like the healthiest man in the world, he began to complain of headaches. A doctor couldn't find anything wrong. But the headaches got worse. And there were spells of dizziness. One day in February, when he was rehearsing for an appearance with the Los Angeles Philharmonic, he got so dizzy he almost fell off the platform. Paul Mueller, who suspected the trouble was really being caused by an electrically wired headband George had taken to wearing because it was supposed to help stop his hair from thinning, leaped to the stage and grabbed hold of him.

"I'm all right, Paul," George told him. "I think I just lost my balance for a minute."

But George was not all right. That evening, while he was

playing the piano in the *Concerto in F*, he missed a few notes and felt himself blacking out. When that happened, he thought he smelled something "like burning rubber." There were a few other episodes of that kind, but once again a physical examination resulted in a report that there was nothing wrong with him.

The headaches grew worse. George became irritable a lot of times, which was not like him, and tired easily, which was even less like him. He kept pressing Paulette Goddard to leave Chaplin and become his wife, but she kept turning him down.

George consulted other physicians, a neurologist, and a famous psychoanalyst named Gregory Zilborg. He was sent to Cedars of Lebanon Hospital in Los Angeles for tests and sent home again. For a while the headaches eased up and he felt better. But soon he began spilling things, tripping on the stairs, fumbling at the piano keys. Friends who visited were shocked by how bad he looked, how pale he was. Once he even tried to push Paul Mueller out of a speeding car. Later he couldn't understand why he had tried to do that.

On Friday, July 9, 1937, George spent the morning at the piano. Around five in the afternoon he decided to lie down for a nap—from which he never woke up: the nap turned into a coma.

That evening, George was rushed to Cedars of Lebanon Hospital. A neurosurgeon, Dr. Carl Rand, examined him. It seemed clear now that the problem was a brain tumor. It would be necessary to operate. The doctor everybody wanted to perform the operation was one of the greatest American neurosurgeons, Dr. Walter Dandy, connected with Johns Hopkins in Baltimore.

The trouble was, nobody could reach Dr. Dandy—at the hospital, his home, his office—anywhere. By this time George Gershwin was a national treasure. His life had to be saved. A frantic search began to find Dr. Dandy. One of George's friends even called the White House to help out.

July 9 had turned into July 10 as two navy destroyers were sent out to find Dr. Dandy, who, it was learned, was enjoying a vacation somewhere on Chesapeake Bay on his yacht.

Finally the yacht was located. Once ashore, accompanied by a motorcycle escort, Dandy was conveyed at high speed to Cumberland, Maryland. There he talked on the phone to the Los Angeles doctors, while arrangements were made for a private plane to fly him out west.

Meanwhile, even as Dr. Dandy made his way to Newark Airport in New Jersey on a smaller plane from Cumberland, Dr. Howard Naffziger, another famous neurosurgeon, who happened also to be on vacation—at Lake Tahoe in California, without a telephone—was found and brought to George's bedside. He decided that the patient's condition was so bad he would have to operate immediately.

It took an hour and a half to locate the tumor, followed by two hours in the x-ray room and five hours of surgery by a skilled team of doctors. But it was hopeless.

At 10:35 on the morning of Sunday, July 11, 1937, the musical genius that had been Gershwin was dead.

Some of the family thought George had survived the operation. In Los Angeles, Ira's wife, Leonore, couldn't bring herself to tell her husband the truth.

George's body was brought back to New York. The funeral service was held at Temple Emanuel. More than three thousand people, many of them great names in the worlds of entertainment and the performing arts, crowded into the sanctuary. A similar service was held at B'nai B'rith Temple in Hollywood. George was buried at Mount Hope Cemetery in Hastings-on-Hudson, north of New York City.

There was a moment of silence the morning of George's funeral in the Hollywood movie studios in memory of George. Then the cameras started grinding again.

19

"Their Music's Here to Stay"

George had not quite finished the score for the movie *The Goldwyn Follies*, which contains four songs by him and Ira, including the last song they ever wrote together, "Love Is Here to Stay." It was Vernon Duke who was called in by producer Samuel Goldwyn to put the rest of the music together.

Gershwin tunes never before published are still being discovered. After his death enough of them turned up to supply the score for the movie musical *The Shocking Miss Pilgrim* in 1947. In 1951 the movie musical *An American in Paris*, which won the Academy Award as best picture of the year, had an all-Gershwin score. A number of Gershwin songs also turned up in the movie of *Funny Face*, starring Fred Astaire, in 1957. It is said there are enough Gershwin songs in the archives to supply the music for several more musicals if the right book and lyrics can be found to match them.

Ira went on to write more great songs with other composers, supplying the lyrics for many a hit musical, including

Rose Gershwin with George in California, 1936

the clever ballads in Moss Hart's *Lady in the Dark,* which he
wrote with the composer Kurt Weill. Ira died in his sleep in
his Beverly Hills home on August 17, 1981. Arthur Gershwin
lived to be eighty. He died on November 20, 1981.

Sometime after George's death, his mother, Rose, decided
she would dictate her memoirs. They proved to be full of
wishful thinking. She claimed that when George was three,
he was already taking music lessons. She had wanted, she
said, for him to be a musician from the start. Of course none
of it was true, and the person she was deceiving was herself.
She decided after a while to give up the idea of writing an
autobiography. Rose Gershwin died in December 1949.

In the fifty years before *Porgy and Bess* made it to the Metropolitan Opera House, it was seen in most of the capital cities of the world. It was taken on a state department tour through the United States, Canada, South America, and Europe from Paris to Moscow (the story of how *Porgy* came to Moscow is told in a wonderfully amusing book by Truman Capote called *The Muses Are Heard*), and all the way to the Middle East. When it played at La Scala in Milan, a performance was interrupted by applause for the first time in that opera house's two-hundred-year history. George had predicted from the first that his opera would make its way.

When *Porgy and Bess* finally opened at the Met on that cold Wednesday evening in February 1985, the Gershwin clan was represented by Ira's widow, Leonore; his sister, Frankie; Arthur's widow, Vicki, and their son, Marc; and Frankie's three children—all in their forties by then—her son, Leopold Godowsky III, and her daughters, Judy and Alexis.

Once again, more than half a century after the Theater Guild production, the reviews were mixed, but *Porgy*'s arrival at the Metropolitan Opera House was a landmark event in American musical history, a symbolic tribute to the genius of its composer.

How to account for that genius? Edward Jablonski and Lawrence D. Stewart wrote in their book, *The Gershwin Years*, that "all attempts to account for either [George] or Ira fail. Their genes? Their Russian origins? Their Jewish tradition? . . . All are explanations that explain nothing."

Yet in an article called "What Is Jewish About the Music of George Gershwin?" his first biographer, Isaac Goldberg, did try to explain. He put it like this: "Naturally, having been born of Jewish parents, Gershwin inherits whatever is heritable of the Jewish body and mind. Having been reared in an environment predominantly Jewish, he received the social heritage of the average New York Jew in the early days of this century. I doubt that he ever spent much time in a synagogue, where he could have grown up amid the liturgical chants. Jewish folk-music, on the other hand, he must have heard plenty. Just as Yiddish intonation and Yiddish expressions have entered into the very language of the Eastern American, so have certain elements of Jewish folk songs made their way, largely through Tin Pan Alley, into American popular song. This has not been part of a conscious program. It has taken place in the way that all cultural interchange takes place. It is one of the most natural things in the world."

The key word here is *natural*. Out of the Yiddish musical theater on Second Avenue, which George certainly attended as a youngster, came the musical theater of Broadway. It is no coincidence that the names of the most famous composers on Broadway and in Hollywood who wrote America's songs have been Jewish; not only George Gershwin but Jerome Kern, Irving Berlin, Jule Styne, Jerry Herman, Morton Gould, Harold Arlen, Leonard Bernstein, Kurt Weill, Frank Loesser, and others, right down to Stephen Sondheim. Out of the chants of the Hassidim, out of the sentimental melodies of the ghettos of Eastern Europe, out of the vast treasury of Jewish music enriched over thousands of years during the wanderings of Jews from land to land, came the songs these composers wrote.

Once, an old friend stopped Jerome Kern on the street and asked. "What are you doing these days, Jerry?" and Kern answered: "Still busy writing Jewish songs." George Gershwin might have said the same. He didn't have to go out and study Jewish music, although he did that too when he was getting ready to make an opera out of *The Dybbuk*. It was already part of him. The chants of the synagogue can be found not only in the sketches he jotted down for that opera, but in songs like "My One and Only," in the "blue" notes that occur in black jazz and in Hassidic chants as well, and everywhere in *Porgy and Bess*. As Goldberg remarks, "Hear a Negro sing the tune and it sounds, so to speak, black. Hear a Jew sing it . . . and it takes on a decidedly Jewish complexion."

In any case, while the tunes of countless less inventive composers lie forgotten in the vaults of American music, most of us still go along with the songwriters Burton Lane and Ralph Freed, "I like a Gershwin tune, How about you?"

What might he have gone on to accomplish had he lived beyond the age of thirty-eight?

Over the years since his death, there have been many tributes to George. A Broadway theater bears his name. In 1973, to commemorate the seventy-fifth anniversary of his birth, the U.S. Postal Service put out a special postage stamp in his honor. Only a year after he died, Warner Brothers in Hollywood started planning a memorial movie. Five screenwriters, including the famous playwright Clifford Odets, worked on the script. The movie that came of all this, *Rhapsody in Blue*, starred Robert Alda (the father of Alan Alda, the star of *M*A*S*H*), who looked remarkably like George. The part of George had almost gone to the young Leonard Bernstein. Alda played the part well, but on the whole it was not a very good movie and certainly had little to do with the real story of George or the rest of the Gershwins.

In 1987 there was talk of a new movie to be produced by Martin Scorsese, with David Mamet to write the script and possibly Robert DeNiro to play George. A revival of *Lady, Be Good!* at the Goodspeed Playhouse in Connecticut opened to rave reviews. A revival of *Strike Up the Band*, restoring everything including songs cut out of the original, was staged in Philadelphia in 1985. Director Peter Sellars, former head of the Kennedy Center in Washington, used Gershwin music in an unusual way as part of a production of a play by the Russian playwright Maxim Gorky.

In 1986, Maryland Public Television produced a 90-minute program about George Gershwin. Actor William Hurt narrated, Leslie Uggams sang Gershwin songs, and Burton Lane and others played the piano and talked about George's style. George's sister, Frankie; Ira's widow, Leonore; Mabel Schirmer; Kay Swift; and others who had known and worked with

George were on hand to take part in the tribute. Other television specials followed, notably a 90-minute public television American Masters production called "Gershwin Remembered." The show featured just about everybody who had ever known him and included a generous helping of musical segments.

There was a Gershwin evening at the White House.

When *Porgy and Bess* was performed in a new production staged by Trevor Nunn at the Glyndebourne Festival in England for the first time in the summer of 1986, the audience gave it a ten-minute ovation, and the critics raved. The *Daily Telegraph* called it "a major success." The *Guardian* declared it "likely that Glyndebourne will never have a triumph like this again."

There were Gershwin gala concerts, revivals of musicals including *Of Thee I Sing*, and *Let 'Em Eat Cake*, television and radio specials, and musical tributes of every kind to mark the fiftieth anniversary of George's death in 1987. That year, too, playwright Neil Simon announced he was working on a new musical called *A Foggy Day*, to be set in London and Vienna in 1933 and featuring classic songs by the Gershwin brothers.

On February 25, 1986, that year's special honor, the Trustees Award, was presented to Ira's widow, Leonore, at the Grammy Awards broadcast in Los Angeles. Handing the award to Mrs. Gershwin, Barbra Streisand pointed out that George's music is as alive today as when he and Ira started writing their songs in the 1920s.

That same year, Barbra Streisand's own best-selling album of Broadway music included songs from *Porgy and Bess*. Linda Ronstadt recorded several Gershwin songs. The musical *My One and Only*, featuring Gershwin music, was touring the country. "I Got Rhythm," "Summertime," and the blues theme from *Rhapsody in Blue* were being used in television commercials by companies like Volvo, Toyota, Estee Lauder, and Duncan Hines cake mix. As one music company executive put it, "It's very clear, their music's here to stay."

In March 1987, it was announced that eighty crates of music stored for years in a Warner Brothers warehouse in Manhattan had been opened, containing hundreds of songs, many previously unknown, by Jerome Kern, Victor Herbert, Richard Rodgers—and George Gershwin. There were seventy lost Gershwin songs, many with lyrics by Ira. The discovery made front page news. One music-theater historian compared it to opening King Tut's tomb in Egypt. Among the Gershwin finds were the missing original scores of the musicals *Primrose, Tip-Toes,* and *Pardon My English.*

There have been other gifted American composers; there has never been another George Gershwin. At a memorial broadcast for him, the composer Arnold Schoenberg, whose difficult music is different in every way from that of Gershwin, said of his friend, "Music to him was the air he breathed, the food which nourished him, the drink that refreshed him. Music was what made him feel, and music was the feeling he expressed."

"Directness of this kind is given only to great men," Schoenberg went on, "and there is no doubt that he was a great composer. What he achieved was not only to the benefit of a national American music but also a contribution to the music of the whole world."

In Nazi Germany, George's music was banned along with all else Jewish, including the Jews themselves. Since World War II, Gershwin's music has been played by German orchestras under great Jewish conductors such as Leonard Bernstein.

People the world over still listen with pleasure to the music of George Gershwin.

LISTENING TO GERSHWIN

In recent years, there has been a revival of interest in Gershwin's music, and you may have heard some of it. If you would like to hear more, there is a great deal of Gershwin on records and tapes, but it is not always easy to know which version of a piece to choose, either at a music store or at the local public library.

Gershwin wanted to create a fresh new music rooted in America—the music of the people, if there was such a thing, including jazz, and to give it form and shape so that it would last despite changing musical fashions. He was not the only American composer who tried to do this, but what he wrote is so much his own that there has been no one as yet to take his place.

You might start with an album recently issued by RCA called *Gershwin Plays Gershwin* (RCA AVM1-7114, cassette ALK1-7114). Here is the original recording of *Rhapsody in Blue* with Paul Whiteman and his Concert Orchestra, in the first Ferde Grofé arrangement, with the composer at the piano.

There are many cuts, including most of the middle section, but you will get a good idea of how this work sounded when it was first performed and of Gershwin's own energetic style at the keyboard. On the same program, you can also hear him playing three of his piano preludes and a number of the songs from *George Gershwin's Song Book*. This collection also contains the first recording of *An American in Paris* under Nathaniel Shilkret, and if you listen carefully enough you might even be able to make out the sound of George himself at the celesta before he was asked to leave the studio.

The entire Aeolian Hall concert of February 12, 1924, Paul Whiteman's "Experiment in Modern Music" that launched *Rhapsody in Blue*, can now be heard on recordings in two reconstructed versions. *The Birth of the Rhapsody in Blue* (Music Masters, two LPs, 201313X; one cassette, 40113–4; CD 60113–4) is a painstaking recreation of the original concert conducted by Maurice Peress on the basis of scores from the Whiteman Archives; the other version obtainable from the Smithsonian Institution in Washington, D.C. (The Smithsonian Collection, two discs DMM2 0528), is made up of period recordings with Gershwin himself as soloist in the *Rhapsody*. It can be ordered from the Smithsonian Collection, R 028, Smithsonian Customer Service, P.O. Box 10230, Des Moines, Iowa 50336. Both albums are fascinating, though the sound on the Smithsonian recording is of course quite dated, and the *Rhapsody* is the same abridged performance to be heard on RCA. Neither precisely mirrors the original concert.

The fact is, maybe because he had too practical a knowledge of show business and of the attention span of audiences, and was so anxious for his work to please the public, Gershwin frequently allowed cuts and alterations in his work not only when performed on stage and in the concert hall, but when recorded too. Partly because in his time a record only lasted about four minutes per side, he permitted those drastic cuts in the *Rhapsody* as well as in early recordings of the *Concerto in F* and other works. Even after his death and the invention of the LP, when Columbia set out to record *Porgy and Bess* complete for the first time, it turned out not to be so complete after all. The conductor, Lehman Engel, had to cut about half an hour out of it so it would fit on six LP sides. Only now is it possible to obtain uncut versions of all Gershwin's serious compositions, restored to their original length and to the way he wanted them to sound in the first place— before musicians less talented than himself were allowed to tamper with them.

The complete works for orchestra and for piano and orchestra, with the St. Louis Symphony under Leonard Slatkin and with Jeffrey Siegel at the piano, are available on the Vox label (three discs, SCBX 5132; three cassettes, C6X 5332). This collection contains *Rhapsody in Blue*, the *Second Rhapsody*, "*I Got Rhythm*" *Variations*, the *Concerto in F*, the *Cuban Overture*, *Lullaby for String Orchestra*, the *Catfish Row* suite from *Porgy and Bess*, *An American in Paris*, and *Promenade*. Siegel's playing is not always as jazzy and spirited as it might be, but at least the music is all there and the recorded sound is wonderful.

Both Frances Gershwin and Gershwin authority Edward Jablonski favor the recordings made with pianist Werner Haas and the Orchestra of the National Opera of Monte Carlo under Edo de Waart. Most of these have been made available on a single cassette which plays for 86 minutes (Philips, 416–220–4) and contains *Rhapsody in Blue*, Robert Russell Bennet's *Porgy and Bess* suite (which is not as exciting as Gershwin's own), *An American in Paris*, the *Cuban Overture*, the "*I Got Rhythm*" *Variations*, and the *Three Preludes*. Haas also recorded the concerto, but this seems to be out of print. I find his playing a little bland, but he does put the music rather than his own personality first, and this is a good thing. Livelier treatments can be found in the recordings pianist Earl Wild made with Arthur Fiedler conducting the Boston Pops for RCA (two discs, VCS 7097; double-play cassette, CRK2–0783), including the *Concerto in F; An American in Paris*, *Rhapsody in Blue*, the *Porgy and Bess* suite and the "*I Got Rhythm*" *Varia-*

tions. Michael Tilson Thomas, who claims to have restored the *Second Rhapsody* to the way Gershwin intended it to sound before arrangers tampered with it, has recorded that work along with *Rhapsody in Blue*, all five of the preludes, and several newly discovered Gershwin show tunes (CBS compact disc, LP, or cassette, IM 39699). Thomas conducts from the keyboard and the performances are pretty exciting. So are a number of Gershwin performances with Leonard Bernstein playing and conducting (CBS, M 31804; cassette MT 31804).

The wide-awake recordings pianist Oscar Levant made of Gershwin's concert works have been re-released by CBS Records in all three formats—CD, LP, and cassette. The program includes his versions of the *Three Preludes*, the *Rhapsody in Blue* with the Philadelphia Orchestra under Eugene Ormandy, the *Second Rhapsody* and *"I Got Rhythm"* Variations with Morton Gould and His Orchestra, and the *Concerto in F* with the New York Philharmonic conducted by Andre Kostelanetz (CD FM 42514, LP MK 42514, and cassette FT 42514). The recorded sound has been remastered and vastly improved, and the pianism still sparkles. The greatest recording I know of both the *Concerto* and *Rhapsody*, with the kind of high-strung, brilliant, sassy playing no other pianist has come near, was made for RCA by Jesus Maria Sanroma with the Boston Pops under Fiedler. It was around for a while as an LP on the RCA Camden label (CAL-304). Perhaps RCA will reissue it some day and you will get a chance to obtain it. Meanwhile, try a library collection.

The most luxurious-sounding Gershwin collection of all features Phillippe Entremont at the piano with Eugene Ormandy conducting The Philadelphia Orchestra (two discs, CBS MG-30073; two cassettes, Odyssey CBS; 90-minute cassette, MGT 30073). The contents include the *Concerto in F, Rhapsody in Blue, An American in Paris,* and *Porgy and Bess— A Symphonic Picture.*

For the complete *Porgy and Bess*, nothing yet has surpassed the Houston Grand Opera production on RCA (three discs or three compact discs, ARL-3, three cassettes, ARK3-2109). Another complete *Porgy* is Lorin Maazel's on London (three discs, 13116; three cassettes, 5–13116). The singers are not always as convincing as the group in the Houston production, but the Cleveland Orchestra and chorus sound sensational. Simon Estes, who played Porgy in the Metropolitan Opera production, can be heard with other singers in a program of selections (Philips LP and compact disc, 412720–1; cassette, 412720–4). Some *Porgy* enthusiasts swear by Leontyne Price's Bess and William Warfield's Porgy in another recording of highlights (RCA record or cassette, AGL1–5234), but I say, if you're going to listen to an opera, why not enjoy the whole thing instead of just bits and snatches! Excerpts from the not quite complete version on Odyssey under Lehman Engel, with a fine singing cast, can be heard on a single cassette (Odyssey, YT-35501); it is also still obtainable in the longer version (Odyssey three discs, 32360018E).

The opera *Blue Monday*, along with two madrigals and two art songs by Gershwin and the choral scene from *Let 'Em Eat Cake* all recorded with the Gregg Smith Singers, may be found on Turnabout (34638; cassette Vox, CT 2103.638). If you're fortunate enough to dig it up, you can hear an earlier version of *Blue Monday* with Skitch Henderson conducting a concert version with an excellent unnamed all-black cast, recorded at Philharmonic Hall in New York on May 20, 1968. On the same record you can hear a legendary broadcast of *Rhapsody in Blue* with Earl Wild on piano, Benny Goodman on clarinet and Arturo Toscanini conducting the NBC Symphony, recorded on November 1, 1942. This also has the premiere of the *"I Got Rhythm" Variations* with the New York Philharmonic conducted by Artur Rodzinski on October 8, 1944. As a bonus, there is the voice of Bobby Short singing "Mischa, Yascha, Toscha, Sascha" as recorded on November 14, 1971 (Penzance Records, 43, occasionally obtainable from Darton Records in New York).

If you'd like to hear a piano roll of Gershwin himself playing "Rialto Ripples," "On My Mind the Whole Night Long," and "Tee-Oodle-Um-Bum-Bo," and rehearsing scenes from *Porgy and Bess* with members of the original Broadway cast including Edward Matthews, Ruby Elzy, and Todd Duncan and more is available on Mark56, 667.

The jazziest treatment available of *George Gershwin's Song Book*, outside of the composer's own, mentioned above, is pianist William Bolcom's (Nonesuch record or cassette, 71284). You might also want to sample Kevin Cole, who has a fine feeling for Gershwin's piano music. He can be heard playing tunes from *Primrose; Lady, Be Good!; Girl Crazy;* and a number of neglected Gershwin tunes in *Unknown Gershwin* (Fanfare, DFL 7007; cassette DFC 7007).

If you want to hear the *Rhapsody* uncut in its pared-down setting for piano and jazz band the way Gershwin originally conceived it, listen to Eugene List at the piano with the Berlin Symphony under Kurt Adler (Turnabout record or cassette, 34457).

Gershwin's brilliant overtures to his musical comedies can be heard by the Boston Pops under Arthur Fiedler (London, 411835; cassette, 411835–4); by Eric Kunzel and the Cincinnati Pops (Turnabout, 34749; cassette, CT-2250) or, most of them the way they probably sounded before the fancy arrangers took over, by Michael Tilson Thomas and the Buffalo Philharmonic (CBS record or cassette, M-34542).

When it comes to the popular Gershwin, the possibilities are endless. You can hear Barbara Hendricks singing his songs (and arias from his operas) accompanied by the duo-pianists Katia and Mariella Labeque (Philips, 9400; cassette, 7300). Sarah Vaughn is captured just as she sounded at a live concert with Michael Tilson Thomas conducting in highly emotional treatments of song after song (CBS, 73650; cassette, MT 32405). Practically every famous pop singer in the world at one time or another has recorded an album of Gershwin or included a number of songs on a program. My own favorite is *Ella Sings Gershwin,* two cassettes obtainable on the Book-of-the-Month Club label (Book-of-the-Month Club Classics Record Library, two cassettes, 20–5252) with Ella Fitzgerald interpreting every song with cool grace and style. Joan Morris, with William Bolcom at the piano, works a lot of spirit and humor into *Songs by Ira and George Gershwin* (Nonesuch disc or cassette, 1358). And you can hear how Frankie Gershwin put her small voice to big use in *Frances Gershwin—For George and Ira* on Monmouth Evergreen (MES/ 7060).

Such terrific entertainers as Barbara Cook, Bobby Short, Elaine Stritch, and Anthony Perkins sing thirteen unfamiliar Gershwin tunes, including "There's More to the Kiss than the X-X-X" and the "Scandal Walk" from the *Scandals of 1920* on Ben Bagley's *George Gershwin Revisited* (Painted Smiles, 1357); then there's *Gershwin Rarities* with Kaye Ballard, Nancy Walker, and others (Citadel, 707).

Some record companies have gone to a great deal of trouble to round up fine Broadway casts and reconstruct what Gershwin's music sounded like on Broadway in show albums, or have issued albums of movie soundtracks or original cast recordings. Outstanding examples are the new recordings of *Of Thee I Sing* and *Let 'Em Eat Cake,* featuring full singing casts headed by Maureen McGovern, Larry Kert, and Jack Gilford, with the Orchestra of St. Luke's and the New York Choral Artists, Michael Tilson Thomas conducting (CD two discs M2K 42522, two LPs S2M 42522, two cassettes S2T 42522); *Girl Crazy,* with Mary Martin and others (Columbia, CSP COS-2560E); *Funny Face,* the movie, with Fred Astaire and Audrey Hepburn (Stet, DS-15001); *Heritage of Broadway, Music of George Gershwin* (Banner Bainbridge, 1012); Gershwin music from Woody Allen's movie *Manhattan* (Columbia disc or cassette, JS 36020); Gershwin songs from the show *My One and Only* with Twiggy and Tommy Tune (Atlantic, 80110-1, cassette 80110-4); *Oh Kay!* with the cast of the 1960 Broadway production (State, DS-1507) or with Jack Cassidy,

Barbara Ruick, and cast (Columbia, CSP ACL-1050); with Gertrude Lawrence, the composer, and members of the 1926 London and New York casts (Smithsonian American Musical Series, R 001); *Shall We Dance*, with Fred Astaire and Ginger Rogers and cast, taken from the movie soundtrack (Soundtrack, 106); *Lady, Be Good!* with the composer and members of the 1924 cast, including Fred and Adele Astaire (Smithsonian American Musical Series, R 008); *Tip-Toes*, selections from the original 1924 London production (Monmouth Evergreen, MES 7052); and *Of Thee I Sing*, a reissue with Jack Carson, Paul Hartman, and cast (Capitol, T 1161), no longer listed but maybe you can track down a copy.

Happy listening!

FURTHER READING

In the course of preparing this book, my research led me to a number of earlier books and countless articles on the subject of George Gershwin. For further reading and study about George, as well as about Ira and the other members of the Gershwin clan, I feel I can conscientiously recommend the following:

Armitage, Merle. *George Gershwin, Man and Legend.* New York: Books for Libraries Press, 1970.

Capote, Truman. *The Muses Are Heard.* New York: Random House, 1956.

Duke, Vernon. *Passport to Paris.* Boston: Little, Brown & Co., Inc., 1955.

Ewen, David. *George Gershwin: His Journey to Greatness.* Englewood Cliffs, N.J.: Prentice-Hall, Inc., 1970.

Goldberg, Isaac. *George Gershwin: A Study in American Music.* New York: Simon & Schuster, Inc., 1931. With supplemental material by Edith Garson. New York: Ungar Publisher Co., 1958. This was the first published biography.

Hellman, Lillian. *An Unfinished Woman.* Boston: Little, Brown & Co., Inc., 1970. Pages 73–74.

Jablonski, Edward. *George Gershwin.* New York: G.P. Putnam's Sons, 1962.
———. *Gershwin.* New York: Doubleday & Co., Inc., 1987.
———, and Lawrence D. Stewart. *The Gershwin Years.* New York: Doubleday & Co., Inc., 1973.

Kimball, Robert E. and Alfred E. Simon, *The Gershwins.* New York: Atheneum Publishers, 1973.

Levant, Oscar. *A Smattering of Ignorance.* New York: Doubleday, & Co., Inc., 1940.

Rushmore, Robert. *The Life of George Gershwin.* New York: Crowell-Collier, 1966.

Schwartz, Charles. *Gershwin: His Life and Music.* New York: Da Capo Press, 1979
———. *George Gershwin: A Selective Bibliography & Discography.* Detroit: Information Coordinators, Inc., 1974.

INDEX

Page numbers in *italics* refer to illustrations.